SPINSTER NO MORE

A CHRISTIAN HISTORICAL WESTERN ROMANCE

KATHLEEN BALL

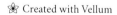 Created with Vellum

CHAPTER ONE

"Quick! Duck into the next alley!" Daire whispered breathlessly over her shoulder.

Brynn's soft-soled shoes allowed every sharp cobble they raced over to shoot agony through her tender feet. Keeping up with Daire was next to impossible, but quitting wasn't an option, so she tried her best to push on. Her life was in Daire's hands.

They turned the corner, and Daire pulled Brynn to hide behind an empty wagon. Their breaths came out in loud pants. They covered their mouths with their hands to subdue the noise.

Brynn stared at the start of the alley, waiting to be captured and dragged back to the asylum. Her heart pounded in her ears and the pit in her stomach grew larger. Tremors or fear rippled through her.

"Let's go but keep as quiet as possible. The store's back door is just around the corner. We'll be safe once we're inside." The apprehension reflected in Daire's eyes didn't look as confident as her words.

Brynn moved cautiously down the alley, hugging the wall.

They paused as Daire peeked around the corner and gave a quick nod.

This was it. Taking a deep breath, Brynn followed her new friend as she turned right and opened a wooden door. They entered and closed it softly then leaned against it, both drawing in deep breaths.

A large woman bustled toward them. Her eyes widened. "What in the world? Daire, is that you? Quick, hide in the storeroom behind the flour barrels." The woman jerked her head toward the storeroom and slowly walked toward the front of the store.

Entering the storeroom, they located the barrels and crouched down behind them.

"Who chased us?" whispered Brynn.

Daire shook her head. "Anyone from the asylum could have been responsible. I was so careful. No one ever glanced at me as I went home before. We'll be fine."

Using her sleeve, Brynn wiped the sweat from her brow. Her hands shook. They hadn't escaped the danger yet. In fact, it seemed far from it.

"How many people have you helped escape?"

Daire's gaze grew serious. "Only you. I'm leaving, we're leaving town in the morning. My brother is helping us. I really didn't anticipate anyone coming after us so quickly. I know they would have found you to be missing at bedtime. Unfortunately, they discovered you left a bit earlier than I planned." Reaching out, she gave Brynn's hand a comforting pat. "But we'll be just fine."

The pounding of her heart persisted, loud and unyielding. Brynn's whole body shook. What had made her think Daire had done this previously?

The door swung open and quickly closed again. "I sent for your brother, Daire. No inquiries about you have been made so far. Either of you."

"Mrs. Beasley, this is Brynn. I'm helping her—"

"I don't want to know. Nice to meet you Brynn, stay safe, both of you." Silently, she closed the door behind her as she left.

Daire sighed. "Cormac will get us to safety. You'll like him."

"Cormac is your brother?"

"He's taking us to North Texas. He has a small ranch there."

Panic filled Brynn. Where was she supposed to go? They never got that far in the escape plan. She had no one to ask for help. She certainly couldn't go home. Squaring her shoulders, she drew a deep breath. No matter what, she'd not let on the fear she felt. Daire had already taken too many risks for her.

The door opened once again. A broad-shouldered man filled the doorway. Just as she was going to make herself as small as possible, Daire touched her shoulder.

"Come on, it's Cormac."

"Hurry, ladies. I have the wagon out back. Get in it." His deep voice brooked no argument. Before Brynn even got a good look at him, he was gone.

The women hurried out the door they'd just entered through and flung themselves into the back of the covered wagon.

"Yaw!"

Brynn fell to the side as the wagon jerked forward. The space around them was cramped. A great many items needed for the trip north seemed to be packed inside. Where did they plan to drop her off?

Lord, here I am again, asking for Your divine intervention. Please help me find a safe place. You have answered my pleas by getting me out of that place. Thank You. Please don't allow Daire and Cormac to come to any harm because of me. Amen.

·   ·   ·

WHEN THEY WERE JOLTED by bumps and dips of the wagon, it became clear they had departed from the main road. A sigh of relief finally came. At this moment, her safety was all she could hope for.

"Thank you, Daire. I didn't realize how big of a risk it was to get me out of there. I have never met a woman as brave as you. No matter where your travels take you, I wish you and your brother all the best."

Daire smiled. "It sounds like you're about to leave. I had hoped you'd come with us. A new life in the North of Texas could be the answer to your problem."

Brynn reached out and firmly grasped Daire's hand. "Do you mean it? A new life is the only answer for me. I can't go back. They'll just put me back in the insane asylum. It's unbelievable that my future mother-in-law placed me there and I'm still in shock. How is it possible for something like that to happen?"

The wagon went over another bump, and they released hands to hold onto the side.

Suddenly the wagon halted, and Brynn could relax her tense muscles for a moment. Holding on so hard to the side of the wagon left her hands aching.

In an instant, Cormac stood at the back of the wagon, hastening them to come out that way.

He swung Daire down and then he turned his gaze on Brynn. He was indeed wide shouldered, but it was his gray eyes that drew her attention. They held compassion within them, and it was everything she needed.

Lifting his arms, he placed his hands on either side of her waist and lifted her down. His smile sent a jolt through her. Being on her guard around him would be advisable. She'd never met a man she could trust.

CHAPTER TWO

"It was too dark to drive the horses any further," Cormac said as he assessed both women. Despite the escape not going exactly as planned, they seemed to be holding up well.

"Come, let's get a fire going and then we can sleep around it. We don't have enough light to put up the tent and as you saw there isn't enough room in the wagon. There's jerky if you're hungry. I hadn't planned to light out so quickly."

They all gathered firewood, and he started the fire. As they settled around it, Daire handed out a blanket to each of them.

"Tell me what happened. Thomas came to get me and all he said was his ma sent for me." Cormac gazed at his sister and then at Brynn. Brynn's complexion was pale, and her face appeared too thin. Why had she been placed in an asylum? What had she done?

"It went as planned," Daire started. "But someone followed us. It became a chase, and we were lucky to get away."

"I'm glad you did."

"I'm glad you packed and were ready to go," his sister commented.

Brynn sat very still and silent.

"It's fortunate you were able to leave with Mrs.—"

"Thistle, her name is Brynn Thistle."

"You can call me Brynn," Brynn's voice quivered.

"Daire explained she hadn't been able to tell you any of our plans until now. I hope they are acceptable to you?" He patiently waited while she stared at her hands and then at the fire.

"I do know we are traveling to North Texas. If I'm not mistaken, she said you own land there."

This time, she cast a brief glance in his direction. Caution filled her blue eyes.

"The safest way to travel is in a group. Hopefully, nobody will come searching for you and it's safer to be in a larger group of wagons. Apart from my sister's interest in you, I am completely clueless about your circumstances. I hope the trip won't be too grueling for you. You could always sit in the wagon instead of walking if necessary."

Her eyes narrowed. "I will walk, Mr. O'Neill, if that is satisfactory to you. I'm stronger than I look. I wasn't in that... that *asylum* for very long. They didn't have time to starve me yet."

"Call me Cormac." He shook his head. "Starved?"

Brynn turned away from him and stared into the fire again.

"It's a horrible place, Cormac. I don't want to get into it all tonight, but withholding food from certain inmates was common," Daire explained.

He furrowed his brow. What *was* that place? "I have jerky," he offered.

"Thank you, but I'm so tired," Brynn explained, shaking

her head slowly. "I appreciate the offer, though. We'll be safe here tonight?"

"We're on property a friend owns. We'll be fine. Shuteye will do us all good. Night." He rolled the blanket and stowed it under his head. Was it the right choice to take Brynn with them? He should have asked his sister more questions. Only time would tell.

———

UPON OPENING HER EYES, Brynn promptly shut them again. Waking in unfamiliar surroundings shook her. Slowly, she opened her eyes again. Outside was good, wasn't it? She froze when she heard a man's voice. It was Cormac, she realized as the events of the previous day rolled through her memory. Inhaling deeply, twice, she calmed herself and turned her head.

Daire and Cormac were whispering. Cormac wore a thunderous expression on his face. As he turned his head, their gazes collided. His expression didn't change. In fact, he scowled at her.

Brynn sat up. "Good morning."

Cormac slapped his hat against his leg and then stormed off.

A lump formed in her throat.

"Daire, he doesn't want me to come with you, does he?"

"He'll get over it. In one way he's right. We know little about you. I know you shouldn't have been at the asylum." Daire offered a hesitant smile.

Brynn stood, folded her blanket, and carried it to the wagon. "It's a simple story. I'll wait for your brother to come back and tell you both. Meanwhile, I'm starving."

Daire smiled. "Let's get breakfast made. That should put Cormac in a better mood."

"Only if there's coffee involved," Cormac said from behind her.

Brynn jumped, putting a hand to her heart. With a sudden twist, she pivoted and locked eyes with him. "You scared me. As for my background, I was uninteresting until my father died. I ran my father's household and then it became mine. Having something valuable attracts many people who suddenly aspire to be your friend. I'll fill you in while we eat."

Nodding, he walked over to the fire and threw in more wood.

Men wanted meek and mild. She'd learned that much growing up. Meek and mild, her first lesson at the asylum. A shiver ran down Brynn's spine. She would never again allow anyone to treat her the way she had been treated. *Tortured* was a more fitting word and thanks to the good Lord Daire had rescued her before the situation worsened.

CHAPTER THREE

*U*ninteresting? She wasn't the type of gal who stood out, but uninteresting? Her blue eyes were pretty, and her hair gleamed. She wore the ugly, shapeless gray dress the asylum had given her. Her mention of that word piqued his curiosity.

They were finally sitting around the fire, each with a plate in hand. Cormac attempted to sneak a quick look at her without being noticed. It didn't work. Her eyes widened when she caught his glance.

"You want to know why I was at the asylum. My father didn't see a need for me to have a social life. When he died, I didn't know many people except for our pastor. He helped me with the arrangements. Less than a week after the funeral, men arrived at my door, many bearing flowers.

"Shock overwhelmed me. There is a mourning period, but I was told in Texas women were scarce and no one pays attention to such rules. I became overwrought. One woman intervened to offer her support, or so I believed. She appeared to be both kind and extremely knowledgeable. She sat with me during what she dubbed calling hours.

"Then her son came to live with her. In the blink of an eye, Lawrence Thistle became my fiancé and Tracy, his mother, my future mother-in-law. I was completely caught off guard, and it didn't make me happy. I admitted my mistake in accepting his proposal and expressed my desire to end the engagement.

"Lawrence laughed at me. He called me stupid. He warned me I should start behaving like a devoted fiancée if I knew what was good for me. Tracy threatened me, but I didn't take the warnings and threats seriously enough.

"The next thing I knew I woke in a strange room. People knew me as Brynn Thistle, and my mother-in-law labeled me insane. She had permission to confine me there. I know I have never married. Their sole interest was in acquiring the money and possessions that accompanied being married to me.

"Thankfully, Daire, you saved me." With a tight smile and slumped shoulders, her demeanor seemed downcast.

"Did your supposed mother-in-law have the authority to place you in that position?" he asked, his voice rising.

Brynn nodded.

"Happens more than you think," Daire added. "The world is cruel, and that place … If only I didn't have bills to settle."

He lifted his tin cup and took a drink. The coffee was never strong enough unless he made it himself. "I'm sorry you both had a bad time of it." He felt a tight knot in his stomach. He had allowed his sister to reach a state of desperation where she had no choice but to work in that place.

"Don't say it," Daire said. "I know that look. You didn't know there was a debt to be paid. I was completely unaware that Ma had borrowed money until Mr. Perkins showed up and threatened to evict us."

He put the cup down and unclenched his other hand. He'd been busy building his ranch with the expectation of bringing both his mother and Daire to live with him. He should have known, somehow, he should have known.

"I should have—" he started.

"No, it wasn't your fault." The decisiveness in her voice indicated she had no desire to discuss it.

"We'll get packed and on our way. We have an extra day to get to the meeting place, but getting there early just might mean we won't be eating dust the whole way."

BRYNN HELD on to the side of the wagon. Cormac insisted on speaking with his sister and wouldn't let Brynn walk while Daire rode in front. The area was covered in dense forest and rugged terrain. At least for a while, she would be stuck bumping around in the wagon.

Poor Daire. Brynn had neglected to bring up her situation and hadn't thought to inquire about it. How selfish. She should have asked. Then again, there had been little time for conversation. Just plans for escape. Daire would never regret her decision, Brynn promised herself. She would make sure all the work was done. After reaching their destination, she planned to be self-sufficient.

The wagon tilted dramatically to the side, jostling Brynn from her seat and slamming her head against a nearby barrel.

Wincing in pain, she rubbed the side of her head and uttered, "Ouch." She needed to pay more attention and hold on.

All at once, the ride became smoother. What a difference. The gentle rocking motion of the wagon made her drowsy. It reminded her of a cradle.

She woke and looked around, blinking. What was different? The wagon had stopped. Daylight persisted, yet determining the length of her sleep proved impossible. Hastily, she straightened up and smoothed out her unattractive, rough dress.

"Brynn!" Daire called out as she climbed into the back. "We can wash in the stream. I need to gather some soap and clothes. Don't worry, you can borrow something of mine, and we can also makeover my mother's dresses on the trip."

With a gentle touch, Brynn reached out and laid her fingers on her friend's arm. "Thank you. Your kindness is everything to me."

"By showing kindness, we create a cycle where others feel inspired to be kind to us as well."

Brynn smiled. "I like that."

"My mother always said it." Sadness briefly overshadowed her features, but it left when she tugged Brynn's hand. "Come, let's wash up."

Brynn moved toward the rear of the wagon. Startled, she recoiled as hands reached out to offer help. Heat flushed her face. It was Cormac.

Moving toward him, she let him place his hands on either side of her waist. With a swift motion, he swung her down and instantly released her.

"I frightened you again, didn't I?" He flashed her a shy smile.

"I expect it will be a challenge for me to accept help from others." She lowered her head and followed Daire to the water.

IT HAD BEEN a while since he'd had women drying their hair near him. His ranch lacked feminine touches, disregarding the sweeter aspects of life. It was a bit jarring that he hadn't given it much thought. At least they weren't a distraction. His sister and her friend. Was she even a friend?

Although she appeared sane and her story seemed credible, one could never be sure. With men, it was easier; if they backed you in a fight, they were trustworthy. He'd been to war too long for normal thinking. He raised his left shoulder before allowing it to fall.

He trusted Daire. She'd had a hard time, and though she didn't want him to beat himself up because of it, there was no help for it. He shouldn't have waited for his ranch to be built before he contacted her. He had last seen his mother and sister right after the war. He'd given his ma some money with a promise he'd be back for them.

The anticipation of his ma's smile when she saw his house had always sat in the back of his mind. It was a selfish thing, he supposed. If only he'd known.

"What are you chawing on, Cormac? You have the saddest look on your face. It better not be about me," Daire challenged, hands on her hips.

"Can't help it. Right now, I am here, and my plan is to treat you and your Miss—" He cocked his head to the side. "What is your actual surname?"

Brynn jerked her gaze in his direction. "It's Walsh. Clearly not Thistle, but my name *is* Brynn. Given the duration of our time together, using first names seems fitting."

He nodded. "Brynn it is. Maybe we should think of a different last name for you. You probably have people looking for Walsh or Thistle."

Her face fell, and she released a sigh. "Could be right. My mother's maiden name was Price. Would that work?"

"Brynn Price." Daire smiled. "I like it. When do you think we'll meet up with the others?"

"Tomorrow sometime. It's going to be a long day I would imagine. That's why I stopped early today so we could get cleaned up. Which reminds me, it's my turn to get clean clothes and the soap."

CHAPTER FOUR

*C*ormac reined in the horses until the wagon came to a halt, then he patiently waited for an elderly man to approach.

"Howdy!" the man greeted. "I'm Captain Browney. I'm the leader of this here group. Are you the O'Neills, by any chance?"

"Yes sir, I'm Cormac O'Neill."

"Who you got traveling with you?"

"My sister and her friend."

Captain Browney frowned. "Both unmarried?"

"Yes, sir they are. Is there a problem?"

"Why not come down so I can explain?"

Cormac fastened the brake and leaped down from the wagon. "I'd sure like to know what's wrong."

"I have two wagons with soldiers joining us and I don't plan to have unmarried females around. Now your sister I'll allow but a friend. I can't stretch my rule that far." Captain Browney took his hat off and scratched his head. "I wish I could oblige you. You were in the war, weren't ya?"

"Yes sir. I sure was. I wish you'd rethink your rule. I really

14

need to get both women to Northern Texas. I have a ranch there."

All hope left with the captain's shake of the head.

"I'll talk to my sister and figure out our course of action. I'll let you know."

"You don't need to tell me. I'll know when you drive off." The captain put his hat back on and walked away.

He'd have to tell the women they'd be traveling alone. He walked to the back of the wagon and both women were practically hanging out.

"Cormac, what happened? Your expression isn't a good one," Daire said. She always had been perceptive.

"We ran into a bit of a situation. There's a group of soldiers along. He won't take unmarried females. He said he'd take you because you're my sister but not Brynn. We'll be fine. We can make our way ourselves."

Daire's jaw dropped. "You said it was too dangerous," she pointed out.

"I can leave. It's not fair you can't join because of me. What does he expect me to do? Marry one of the soldiers?" A look of terror crossed her face as her eyes grew wider.

"Brynn," he said in a calming tone, "no one expects you to marry a soldier."

"What about a marriage that wasn't real?" Daire asked.

"Nope, that doesn't work for me. Get settled in the wagon, we're ready to go.

Brynn narrowly avoided losing her balance while attempting to leap out of the back of the wagon. He reached and steadied her before she hit the ground.

"Why not tell them I'm married," she insisted.

"I don't think that will work. He already knows you're not. He's not the type of man who falls for tricks easily."

Their gazes collided, and he didn't like the gleam he found in hers.

"You can marry me. We'll just need someone to perform the ceremony."

"Look, Brynn I appreciate the offer, but I will not marry you and then unmarry you. It's not legal. I said we can go alone, and I mean it."

He suppressed a sigh. The stubborn look on her face didn't bode well.

"Cormac," Daire interrupted. "What choice do we have? No one will know about the marriage, and I'm sure if you rip up the marriage papers when we get to your ranch, you'll be fine," she insisted.

"It'll work out somehow, Cormac," Brynn pressed, her voice laced with desperation. "Traveling alone is too much of a risk. I know it won't be as easy as ripping up the papers, but we'll figure it out. This won't be a genuine marriage by any means. You don't have to worry; I won't hold you responsible for any promises."

He turned away. That was the problem. He'd vowed to honor his promises. Especially after all that Daire had gone through trying to make it on her own. Traveling north alone wasn't prudent. The danger was too real for only one man with a gun.

He turned back and stared at his sister. "Fine. Let me find out how we can make this happen." As he walked away, a sense of dread consumed him. What did he know about being a husband? He took back his thinking that a female around would be nice. It would inevitably result in a disaster.

DAIRE RUSHED to Brynn's side. "Are you sure?" Her brow furrowed. "I didn't save you so you could tie yourself to a man you don't know. Not that anything is wrong with my brother, but you should have choices. The Thistles took away your choices, and I don't want that to happen to you again."

Brynn simply nodded, wearing her best, *I'm not foolish or afraid,* smile. "It's really our only course of action. I need to get as far away from that town and that asylum as I can. You and Cormac are the answer to my prayers. Besides, how long can it take to travel to Cormac's ranch?"

Startled by the footsteps behind her, she jumped.

"Anywhere from eighteen days to three weeks," Cormac answered.

Brynn turned around.

"Brynn if you're still willing, there is a preacher in camp who can marry us, but it must be now. His missus is waiting. He was supposed to start their cookfire, and I distracted him. She's not long on patience."

The thumping of her heart quickened as she swallowed hard and offered a resolute nod. "I'm willing."

Brushing her hair and washing her face weren't options, she realized with dismay. She brushed at her dress and patted her hair, but when Cormac sighed somewhat impatiently, she allowed him to take her hand, hurrying her along with his lengthy stride. Daire laughed behind her.

Cormac guided her to a man who seemed far from being a pastor. His brown hat and clothes were tattered, indicating that he had neglected his appearance for quite some time. He wore two gun belts. He must be able to shoot with both hands. But his smile and the expression in his eyes were kind.

"I'm Pastor Martin Crosby, and you must be the gal who wants to marry this here fella."

Her face heated. "Yes, that is me."

"Good, good. Let's get this done. The missus is not happy with me." He winked as if it were an ordinary occurrence.

"Now, I'll say a few words, then you repeat after me, and then I'll pronounce you married. Let's start."

There hadn't been a moment where she could have asked questions, though she didn't have any to ask. Cormac was doing it to protect her. She couldn't have allowed them to travel solo. It would have been a death sentence.

There were so many tribes of Indians in Texas. They were bound to meet up with one, if not more. It wouldn't be fair to Daire or Cormac.

In terms of being a husband, Cormac was not as objectionable as the suitors who had tried to court her. He didn't have any airs about him. It was as though what she saw was what she would get. No pretense of politeness or interest in the latest fashions, not that she was all that interested in clothes, herself.

She'd always had the latest style for church, but otherwise serviceable clothing was best. She wasn't one to need a lot of belongings.

There were so many things she didn't know about Cormac. He seemed like a reasonable enough man. He was good looking. Would he … No, they would be strictly friends. Daire's presence would be a blessing beyond measure for them. They wouldn't have to worry about pretending to like each other. Not that she didn't like him…

"Brynn?"

She jolted out of her musings. "I do."

"I now pronounce you man and wife," Pastor Crosby announced.

Why was she so frequently startled these days? Too much in her own mind. She'd best start paying attention.

Cormac leaned in toward her, and she held her breath. She had never experienced a kiss before. They had drawn a crowd, and they would all be witness to it. Suddenly Cormac turned his head and kissed her cheek.

In that moment, he relinquished her hand, and she felt the loss of his warmth.

"Now we are sisters!" Daire declared before she hugged first Brynn and then Cormac.

"Be happy. The missus is giving me the look which means I'm in the doghouse, but it was worth it."

A few of the crowd introduced themselves and congratulated them. The soldiers approached, and Cormac steered both her and Daire away from the crowd and toward their wagon.

Finally, she felt calm enough to breathe effortlessly.

CHAPTER FIVE

*T*he temptation to ask himself if he was out of his mind arose, but it really wasn't a fair question. It was a duty. A favor, a way to get them all to North Texas. Now, if she didn't start giving him brief looks or batting her eyelashes at him, they'd be fine.

Captain Browney approached and shook Cormac's hand. "Congratulations. You sure found yourself a pretty one. You can drive your wagon over yonder and get settled. We leave in two days. At least that's the plan. I hope you're not a stickler for things being done on a certain timetable because that is something that never happens on these trips. I try my best, but people and other instances can put us off track a bit. So far, I have seen no wife with child so that won't be a consideration."

"We'll be ready when you want us to be," Cormac assured him with a smile and a nod. He continued to smile until the captain was out of sight.

"Is everything all right?" Brynn asked.

"Perfect. We are to pull the wagon over there to be part of the circle. Guess we get to stay."

Brynn gave him a quick nod and walked toward the wagon.

Why was he disappointed? He didn't want her attention. He rubbed the back of his neck, trying to make sense of his emotions, but found no answers. A guy didn't pretend to get married every day.

For pretend it was, a pretend marriage, but he hadn't really given it enough thought. He'd just wanted a quick solution to his problem. Now he had a new type of problem. A man of God had performed the ceremony. That held a distinction for him. Were they lying to God by making this whole thing a farce? Probably, but he needed to put that in the back of his mind. He had his sister to take care of.

AFTER THEY FOUND their spot and unloaded a few of the items they would need right away, Brynn's legs wobbled. She plunked onto a fallen log Cormac had pulled over for them to sit on a little while ago. The last few weeks had been a whirlwind of events for her, leaving her head spinning.

Finding herself committed to a hospital had been life changing. She had found herself there suddenly, with no warning. She'd lost weight, but she hadn't lost her mind. So many of the women there had acted crazy, and they probably didn't start out that way. Were they victims too? If she didn't have to leave, it would have felt wonderful to confront Tracy Thistle and her snake of a son.

Mrs. Thistle was most likely wearing her mother's jewelry and examining everything in the house for its monetary value. There were many fine pieces of jewelry, but her father had told her she had to wait until she was married to wear them. Maybe they hadn't found the hidden safe, but she would not hold on to any hope of that. It would be better to just consider everything to be gone.

Essentially, it was. What a trusting fool she'd been. Ripe for the plucking. She had never been fond of Lawrence, but she had never imagined she'd end up in an asylum. There must be some internal flaw within her that prevented her from seeing people for who they truly were. She usually observed an overwhelming amount of good and a lack of their wrongdoing.

Flaw was harsh. The thought of someone being so sneaky never crossed her mind. Learning that lesson had been exceedingly difficult.

"Daire, why are you looking so worried?"

Daire wiped her hands on her apron and sat down on the log next to her. "You look so forlorn. Cormac is really a good man. I understand that nobody is perfect, and I know you come from a wealthy background and didn't anticipate traveling with people like us—"

"The likes of you? I would never think that. My father had money, not me. He liked to lord over people because he was rich, but he wasn't rich in things that matter. He didn't have love or friends. I only loved him because I had to. My mother never liked him. We never entertained at the house. He wasn't nice to people. Even in church, I could tell the congregation greeted him out of obligation. I don't like that the Thistles have probably stolen everything, but I never intended to be a lady of leisure."

"But—"

Shaking her head, she released a sigh. "I was the housekeeper. I worked all day every day. The only time off I had was when we attended church. Otherwise, I was at my father's beck and call. I couldn't go to bed until he did. I learned the hard way to be up long before him. But I managed. The people who worked for my father were my friends, and I loved every one of them." She lifted her head and met Daire's gaze. "Living on a ranch until I find my way sounds exciting to me. Do you know much about animals?"

Daire smiled. "We grew up on a farm until the war. We'll be a successful addition to the ranch. I hope you stay for a long time."

Despite the pain in her heart, Brynn smiled back.

Together they put together a noon meal and made dough that would rise so they could cut biscuits for supper.

THE TWO WOMEN seemed to work well together. Standing by the fire, they engaged in light-hearted banter. It was great. Daire had a friend. She certainly hadn't had time for friendships while trying to pay off their mother's supposed debts. Too bad he hadn't happened upon the landlord to discuss the debts. Their mother would never have allowed a debt that large.

He'd take care of his sister now, and she wouldn't have to worry. It must have been horrid to work in the asylum. He gave her a lot of credit for going every day.

Brynn cooked from the first morning, but now after learning about her background, that surprised him. She carried herself well and had nice manners, and he could tell she'd gone to school, but her being rich had never occurred to him. She hadn't made a single complaint. Of course, maybe it was too soon to tell. After all, she needed them.

For what it was worth, he planned to make sure they were all friendly. It would serve them well.

They caught him watching them. Daire smiled and waved. He smiled back as he walked toward them.

For the rest of the day, he made sure he didn't pay too little or too much attention to Brynn. He direly needed relaxation and to let things take their course. Right now, he felt tightly wound. Whenever there was an extended period of silence, he felt the necessity to fill it.

"You seem more anxious about this than I am," Brynn commented once they were by themselves. "Just be yourself. I feel it too, but it's not mandatory we talk all the time or spend our time together. It's clear to me you are observing the other men as they gather and engage in conversation. You don't need to be here for my benefit. It's kind of you but knowing what they're discussing would be better in the long term. Oh!" Her eyes widened, and she pressed two fingers across her pink lips. "I know you're already knowledgeable about wilderness travel, so I'm not suggesting you need to learn anything new."

A loud laugh came from inside the wagon. Daire poked her head out. "This is what we'll do, Cormac go make us some friends, we'll need them to get by. Brynn and I will do the same with the women once I get this wagon straightened out. Cormac, just be sure to get enough wood for supper and for tonight." She pulled her head back into the wagon.

Cormac laughed. "The voice of reason." He stood. "Let Daire know I won't overlook the wood." With a hat tip, he made his way toward the men.

Oddly, Brynn's nervousness brought about a sense of calmness in him.

CHAPTER SIX

"*C*an you tell us what the men talked about or is it a secret?" Brynn asked. She had served supper and was the last to sit down.

"Why would it be secret?" Daire asked.

Cormac laughed. "No, we don't have secrets. Someone suggested a secret password, so we didn't shoot the wrong person, but we all agreed we'd know the difference between us and the Indians by the amount of clothes a person wore."

"The meeting was informative, was it?" Brynn chuckled.

"Actually, it is good to know other men's strengths. Who can track and hunt, who can defend us, things like that. We have a few that have never owned a gun. Why that isn't a requirement to join the wagon train is beyond me." His face took on a serious expression. "The captain is right about the soldiers, though. I don't want either of you wandering off alone. They made a lot of noise and commotion in the town they recently visited. It's crucial to be aware of your surroundings in case you come across Indians."

"Makes sense. I have to admit, I don't know how to handle a gun."

"Daire can teach you. She's quite good with a rifle," Cormac told her.

She nodded her agreement. "That sounds like a good idea. What else did they talk about?"

Cormac laughed. "What did you women talk about?"

"Nothing much." Brynn's face heated.

"It doesn't seem to be nothing much."

Daire smiled. "Brynn got a lot of advice about her wedding night."

Brynn snuck a peek at Cormac. It was probably a toss-up who was redder. A silence settled over them, but she was resolute in not being the one to break it.

They made short work of finishing supper, and she collected the empty dishes and began washing them in the warm water she had prepared earlier. She was overwhelmed by the flood of advice she had been given. She did not know what half of it meant. Some women hinted, while others were too informative in their description of what would take place. A shiver went up her spine.

Fortunately, none of that was going to happen. Ever, never ever. They probably thought they were helping, though a few had a smile that didn't seem to be a helpful or concerned smile. It was hard to describe, but it left her with the feeling they were enjoying her discomfort.

"Those women meant well," Daire commented as she grabbed a towel to dry the clean dishes. "I wasn't happy with some of them, though. I was taught to act ladylike. Maybe I shouldn't have been present since I'm not married."

"In case you have forgotten, I'm not having a wedding night."

Daire laughed. "Good thing, or you'd be running in the other direction. It'll be fine. There will be occasions where you'll need to pretend to be a couple. You know, walking together, standing together at church services and the like.

I'll be there too. The decision to marry was a quick one and not everything was thought out, but we'll make the best of it." Her lips twitched. "And witnessing Cormac's face turn bright red was amusing."

"You're right," Brynn admitted. "I didn't give it any thought, but we will muscle through. I was unaware that the journey to the ranch would be this lengthy. Just how big is Texas? I don't know if I've ever seen a map of it. I've heard of certain towns, that's about it. I feel inadequately informed."

"Don't beat yourself up. I have no idea how big Texas is either. I know it's vast. That's the extent of the information I can provide. Oh, and a lot of the terrain isn't easy." She grinned. "We can learn together as we go along."

Brynn reached out and gave Daire's hand a gentle squeeze. "I don't know why you picked me to help, but I thank God every day you did."

"It was easy, you didn't kick me or bite me. I didn't interact with the women until they'd had their treatments. I was in the hall and was asked to sit with you on your first day. You were genuinely confused why you were there. You didn't sound crazy at all."

CORMAC STOOD at the main fire with most of the men. They were passing a jug of whiskey around, but he declined. Getting strange or disbelieving looks didn't bother him at all. He didn't drink.

It bothered him when people started talking about his wedding night. He always thought such things to be a private matter. One remark angered him so much he wanted to punch the soldier. Instead, he left the fire.

He'd need to remind Daire and Brynn not to be near those soldiers. They weren't a decent type of men. Some people he'd fought with had been the same way, but many had been husbands and brothers who had a respect for females.

The women Daire and Brynn talked to were more audacious than he ever expected. The embarrassment on Brynn's face said it all. Although he wanted to assure her, his face heated and probably turned as red as hers. Besides, the timing wasn't right.

Now, should he set up the tent for the women or have them sleep inside the wagon? He'd sleep under the wagon. It didn't matter what anyone thought. It was none of their business.

Drawing nearer to their fire, he saw Brynn jump up, pour a cup of coffee, and present it to him.

"It's the last of it."

He took the cup and sat down. It was a relief to see her face was back to its normal color.

"Thanks for the coffee. The other men were passing whiskey around."

"You don't drink?" Brynn asked.

"Not unless I'm having a bullet dug out. I don't disapprove, it's their right to drink. I just like being clear minded." He glanced away from Brynn and gazed at Daire.

"I know I've brought it up previously, but I can't stress enough how crucial it is for you to stay away from those soldiers. Their lack of respect for women makes it impossible for me to trust them. I was considering putting the tent up, but it would be safer for the two of you to sleep in the wagon. I'll sleep under it."

Both women nodded.

"We can make more room in the wagon by putting the tent outside," suggested Brynn.

"That will help. I rearranged the wagon a bit this afternoon, and I think there will be more room than we had the last two nights," Daire explained.

"I need my bed roll and I'm fine," he added. "Do you need help getting into the wagon?"

He knew the answer by how fast Brynn turned her head away.

He offered a half-hearted smile. "Night."

"Goodnight," both women answered.

THE NEXT MORNING, Brynn carried the wooden bucket to the river. Many of the woman were already there filling buckets of their own.

Their knowing looks caught her off guard. How mortifying. That was it. She would never get married for real. It was overwhelming.

"Brynn, don't let anyone get you down," an older woman told her. "I got wind of the hen party yesterday. I'm Candace Harris. Our wagon is on the left side of yours if you need anything. It's me and my husband Bernie." She directed a stern look at some of the women. "I don't cotton to crude talking."

"Thank you, Mrs. Harris."

"Call me Candace. I don't think anyone is standing on formalities here. Fill your bucket, and I'll walk back with you."

Brynn kneeled on the bank and filled her bucket. Standing, she overheard snippets of conversation that made it clear she was still the subject of their talk.

"Old biddies. Let's stroll back to our wagons." Candace led the way, and soon they walked side by side.

"I remember what it's like to be a new bride. It's a wonderful feeling you want to hold to your heart and not share. You keep those memories. They are helpful during hard times. If you need anything or just want someone to talk to, I'm here. Bring your sister-in-law too. It's always nice to meet others when you're traveling. This is my wagon."

"I'm grateful for your kind words, Candace. Thank you." She smiled. "I'll bring Daire by sometime. Have a good day."

With just a few yards to go, Brynn reached her wagon. Candace had certainly lifted her spirits. Prior to seeing her, Brynn was preparing to head back to the wagon with an empty bucket.

Not being out in the world had left her at a disadvantage. She was at a loss for how to react to those women. The journey of learning was going to be extensive.

CHAPTER SEVEN

$\mathcal{T}$he long-awaited day had finally arrived. Before dawn, the sound of a bugle startled them awake, and they scrambled to eat breakfast. What Brynn wouldn't have given for a cookstove. They managed biscuits, bacon, and eggs. Though the eggs were in short supply.

They had decided it was prudent to make the dough for the biscuits the night before and, in the morning, cook enough for all three meals. They had also soaked the beans overnight. If anyone went hunting, that would always be a pleasant addition. They were told they wouldn't always stop for the noon meal. Daire and Brynn planned to cook extra bacon.

They filled the water barrels on the sides of the wagon and quickly stored everything.

Cormac whistled a tune as he hitched the horses. Almost everyone seemed in good spirits as they waited for the go signal, except for a few unprepared individuals.

Captain Browney quickly went to those wagons, giving advice and warnings. With his commanding demeanor, he swiftly got the unprepared people ready.

"Wagons ho!" was heard, and then the train started out.

Before long, the scorching Texas sun made it hard to breathe freely. Thank goodness for their poke bonnets. Their long sleeves provided some coverage for their skin, but it didn't alleviate the sweat. Brynn was as lifeless as a wet rag, but there was no point in complaining. Besides, Daire had given her sturdy shoes, and even though they weren't the most comfortable, she didn't feel the sharp rocks under her feet.

The cover story Daire and Brynn invented was a simple one. Brynn had kept house for a woman who died, and Daire had worked at the same house as the cook. Poor Mrs. Jones died suddenly, leaving them without jobs. Daire's brother rushed down to gather them. It was love at first sight for Brynn and Cormac, but neither had wanted to admit it until marriage was discovered to be a condition of traveling with the group.

She didn't notice the rock in front of her until her foot kicked it and she stumbled forward. If not for Daire's steadying arm, Brynn would have fallen flat on her face.

"Close call," said her friend.

"Thank you. I've had multiple close calls because my dress keeps whipping around."

"Me too." Daire sighed. "We need to ask someone about it. I noticed the other women have shortened dresses, but how they keep them from winding around their legs, I don't know." Daire smiled. "I'll be glad when we stop. I'm used to being on my feet, but this isn't easy."

"I'm feeling the same except I'm thankful I have shoes to wear and your dress to share. I know you mentioned making over your mother's dresses. After we finish for the day, we can look at them if we have any energy left. I love sewing." Pride filled her. It was her one talent.

"Oh yes, let's do that. It'll be a blessing to have help. Much to my mother's consternation I never got the hang of sewing except hemming. She'd throw up her hands moaning I'd never catch a husband."

They laughed together until Daire's dress got caught in sage brush.

"Oh dear!" exclaimed Brynn, staring in dismay at the hopelessly snagged fabric. They stopped walking and worked together, getting it uncaught without ripping the cloth.

"Oh, I finally caught up to you!" Candace told them breathlessly as she approached. "Bernie wanted me to walk right next to our wagon. I did for a while so he shouldn't complain. You two need to shorten your hems. You'll never get all that dirt off the bottom of your dresses."

They'd had a pleasant visit the day before. The Harrises were from Louisiana, and this was the second part of their venture to North Texas.

Apparently, some of the same people she had traveled with before were also traveling now. Candace's greatest quality seemed to be that she never spoke negatively about others.

Brynn nodded. "We were just talking about that. How do you keep your dress from blowing?"

Candace chuckled. "I can see I'll have my hands busy with the two of you. Have you been on a wagon train before? Did anyone give you advice?" With a gentle smile, she shook her head. "Never mind, I know the answer. Any piece of metal or even a rock in a pinch. You need to weigh the bottom on the dress down. I am glad to see you both have the poke bonnets. Hard to see around you but worth it to keep the sun off your face."

"I would have never thought to weigh the dress down," Daire commented. "I'm sure you have a wealth of wisdom to share."

"I can't claim to be wise, but our journeys have taught me

a thing or two. We're going back to the north of Texas. We were part of a land grant, and it was a disaster. We bought land and four months later found out the land already belonged to someone else. We just got word that we own some property. Not as much as we bought, but since it's ours, we'll take it."

"What an ordeal," Daire commiserated.

"For every mistake you learn a lesson," Candace said.

"What was the lesson?" Brynn asked.

"If it sounds too good to be true, back away." Candace sounded good natured, though it was impossible to see her face with the bonnet on.

———

WHEN THE CAPTAIN gave the signal to call it a night, Cormac let out a sigh of relief. His arms and shoulders ached from driving the wagon and the horses all day. They must have traveled at least twenty miles. The wagon party had been given a brief stop for the noon meal as their only rest.

With careful precision, he maneuvered the wagon into his assigned spot, swiftly unhitched the horses, and escorted them to the nearby water.

Keeping the horses healthy and strong was the most important part of wagon traveling. Without them, they'd be stuck.

He guided them to an area with abundant grass and secured their movement. They would be fine until nighttime, when he'd bring the livestock in the middle of the wagon circle.

He stopped for a moment and watched Daire and Brynn. Their laughter filled the air as they struggled to light the fire. They were executing it correctly, apart from the fact that he was in possession of the flint.

He strolled the rest of the way, enjoying their smiles.

"You need the flint and the char."

"Welcome back," Brynn said with relief. "I was just about to go to see if we could borrow a flint from the Harrises. I didn't see any charred wood in the wagon."

"I keep the charred wood in the front with me. I saw a wagon burn up once. The char was still burning when they put it inside." He went to the front of the wagon, took a piece of char, and placed it beneath their constructed fire. He hit the flint against a piece of metal and the spark lit the char. After skillfully blowing on it, he'd built a roaring fire.

"What's for supper?" Unexpectedly, two frowns greeted him. He shouldn't have asked.

Daire put her hands on her hips. "Brother dear, we will have beans, biscuits, and bacon. You'd best get used to it."

"Did I say one word about not liking it?"

"No, not yet…"

Chuckling, he shook his head. "You can't find me guilty on mere speculation. I shouldn't have asked, seeing as I bought the supplies. You both must be tired from today's journey. We traveled at least twenty miles."

They heard a loud guffaw, and all turned their heads in the direction it came from. Captain Browney approached.

"Just checking to see how you're fairing. I heard what you said, and you were off about ten miles." He pushed his hat back off his face. "But it was good for the first day. Only a couple stragglers and one loose wheel. Tomorrow we'll aim for more miles. If you don't need nothing, I'll say goodnight."

Cormac shook the older man's hand. "Goodnight."

Captain Browney continued on to the next wagon.

The look of dismay on the women's faces probably echoed his own. Only ten miles? It felt like forever. How were they supposed to go farther tomorrow? Would the distance increase every day?

"Ten. Only ten," Brynn whispered.

Daire sat on the ground. "This is bad. Cormac would you fill the bucket with cold water? Brynn's feet are all blistered."

"I'll be fine," Brynn protested.

Cormac picked up the bucket. "Just like the horses we need to keep your feet in good condition."

Walking away, he realized he'd equated Brynn to a horse. His lips twitched.

CHAPTER EIGHT

*H*ow embarrassing to be sitting with her bare feet in a bucket! It was a wonderful feeling, but she had endured worse at the asylum. However, in the civilized world, women were supposed to keep their feet covered.

"Extraordinary circumstances," Daire told her.

She whimpered as she pulled her stockings away from the blisters. She needed them to be better by tomorrow. After all, her feet were like horses' hooves. If he had directed that remark toward another person, she would have erupted in laughter, but today it lacked amusement.

She made herself useful by sewing rocks into the shortened hems. It was hard to watch Daire do the cooking. Cormac cleaned the dishes while Daire put the next day's beans to soak and mixed the biscuit dough.

Daire assured her it was doing her share, but she felt like a lay-about. In fact, women had been committed to the asylum for laziness. Despicable indeed!

"Why are you narrowing your eyes like that?" Cormac asked.

"I was thinking about how a woman could be sent to the asylum for being lazy. The whole place is a travesty." She breathed in deep and slowly let it out. "I am extremely grateful to Daire and you, more than you can imagine."

"She has always been a kind person. I'm upset because my misjudgment resulted in her working there. My mother would have gone hungry rather than borrow money. She would have worked too. If I'd had the time, I would have tried to get the money Daire already paid that swindler." He let out a deep, weary sigh.

"You didn't know. I'm glad she did work there. Who knows what would have happened to me? I still have a fear that they will come after me, lock me up and throw away the key." Keeping her voice from quavering was nearly impossible.

"They can't touch you any longer. You're my wife now." His eyes widened as though he'd said something he shouldn't have.

"I thank you for the protection of your name. Just like a knight in shining armor."

He shifted. "Don't go getting any ideas about me. I can be as ornery as the rest of them. I'm not hero material. I'm just a man trying to get my family safe and my ranch successful. I can take a look at your feet if you want," he offered.

Her face heated as she looked everywhere but at him. "That wouldn't be seemly. Men don't look at women's feet. It's bad enough we had to shorten our hems. It's untoward."

"A puritan, are you?"

Her gaze collided with his.

"Truthfully, I'm spinster material. I've never been to a gathering except for church-related ones. Only because my father wanted to keep up appearances. It would have been my demise to be alone with a man, regardless of the distance.

To be safe, I just stayed with the elderly widows. No trouble to be had with them."

"You didn't feel as though you were missing out on meeting people your own age?"

"When I was twelve, I insisted I was going to a birthday party. My father pulled me out of school. No friends, no parties. He ruled the house with an iron hand. But that's over now. I'm looking forward to our adventure." She attempted to show a smile that looked genuine.

"I'll try my best not to be unseemly. I must admit I might not know all the rules. I'm out of practice talking to females."

"Are you ridiculing me?"

"Of course not. I want you to be comfortable around me. I apologize if my question about your feet came across as inappropriate. They need tending to."

"What mischief have you been up to, big brother?" Daire entered their camp and halted in front of them, hands on her hips, her gaze fixed on her brother. "It'll take a bit for us to get used to each other. I'm certain you'll be putting your foot in your mouth often." She grinned. "I was just at the Harris' wagon seeing what to do for your feet. Candace gave me this jar of some concoction she said would help and she even had bandages. That woman is a wonder."

Daire sat next to Brynn and dried each foot as she removed it from the water. When she opened the jar, they both gagged. The foul odor was something people avoided putting on their bodies, even their feet.

"Are you sure this stuff will work?" Brynn asked, her eyes watering.

"That's what Candace said. I'm sure once it's on, the smell will disappear. Let's at least try it."

Cormac stood and tipped his hat at them. "As fun as this all seems, I have work to do." He skedaddled before they uttered a word.

"I wonder what got into him?" Daire asked.

"Me, I'm afraid. He offered to tend my feet, and I told him it would be unseemly. Unfortunately, my upbringing was quite strict. Puritan was the word he used."

"He called you a puritan?"

"It wasn't meant to be unkind." She gave a rueful smile. "I proceeded to describe how I never attended parties and instead spent church gatherings sitting with elderly widows."

Daire stared, eyes wide, then shook her head. "Let's get your feet taken care of."

She winced as Daire rubbed the concoction on. "It hurts as bad as it smells."

"You might have to travel in the wagon tomorrow. Some of these blisters look bad. Let's just hope this stuff works miracles." She finished bandaging and sat back. "Seeing feet is unseemly?"

Brynn smiled at her, feeling bashful. "It made sense to me. It's a body part."

Daire laughed. "So are your hands."

Brynn joined in with the laughter. Not knowing what was proper or not was a sad state to find oneself in. Oh, did she really say the slightly shortened hems were untoward? No wonder he thought of her as a puritan.

CHAPTER NINE

"*L*isten up, folks! I expect every man to assemble at the main fire for a meeting. We need to assign times for guard duty," Captain Browney boomed.

With wide eyes, Daire turned her head. "Guard duty? Who is going to protect us when you have guard duty?"

"You are," Brynn answered before Cormac could. "You know how to use a gun. Tomorrow, you can teach me, and we can both guard each other."

Rising to his feet, Cormac nodded. "Sounds like a plan. I need to go." He hurried to the group of men. They all turned and looked at him. He must be the last one to arrive.

"Had to explain things to the new missus?" Hugo Turner inquired, a wide smirk adorning his face. Snide remarks were his trademark.

"I'm here now," Cormac answered and turned his attention to the captain.

"Now, we need four men per shift. Four-hour shifts will work. Shift one starts at eight and shift two starts Midnight. We will all be rising at four to leave no later than five. For the last few evenings, we have had the soldiers performing guard duty. Now that everyone knows what this wagon train is about, it's time we added ourselves into the mix. Are there any individuals who do not know how to shoot or do not have a firearm?

All the men turned their heads one way and then the other, waiting for someone to call out. Two of the men hesitantly raised their hands.

"Good, I only have to teach two of you. We have about one-half hour before shift one. Please explain the timetables of traveling and your shift times to your group. Especially the one about getting up. I've been lenient about stragglers but no more. Stragglers attract Indians. They see a wagon alone and they pounce. Many times, attacking one is not enough and it leads to trouble for us all. Stay together."

Cormac hung around long enough to hear the night's guard assignments. He was on first watch. Best be ready on time.

As he approached his wagon, both women looked cozy near the fire. Supper! He'd have to hurry and eat. This would take some getting used to, but like anything else, folks adapted.

"How did the big meeting go?" Daire asked.

Cormac picked up the plate they'd made for him. "Fine, but I was late. Next time I won't be. They think I was late because I had to explain things to the missus." He put a spoonful of beans and salt-pork in his mouth, chewed and swallowed. "I have first shift tonight. It should end about midnight."

When he saw Brynn's face turn a shade of scarlet, he couldn't help but smile. He shifted his gaze and quickly consumed the rest of his meal.

Daire stood, took his plate, and handed him a cup of coffee. "I'll grab the rifle for you." She headed to the front of the wagon. He'd stashed it there that morning.

"Will you be in much danger out there?" Brynn asked. "Never mind, of course you will. Why else would we need guards? Keep a sharp eye and don't fall asleep."

He chuckled. "Is that friendly advice?"

"That and I don't relish becoming a widow so soon. They might have me marry someone else, and frankly you are the cleanest I've seen so far."

Daire handed him the rifle and a handful of bullets.

"Thanks, Daire. Brynn, I'm grateful that you've noted my finer traits." Shooting her a smile, he downed his coffee and then made his way back to the circle.

He had many qualities, didn't he? Of course, he was clean. He never wanted to be as dirty and stinking as when he'd fought in the war. Water had been for drinking, not cleaning.

"O'Neill, you'll be in the north position. I expect you all to know your compass points. If there's trouble, shoot into the air and let us know. Then get inside the circle, warn people to get out of their wagons and we will all fight with the wagons giving us cover." Each man received a stern gaze from Captain Browney before he nodded.

"Captain, sir, I'm west. Now would that be to my left or my right?" Sebastain Peterson asked.

Cormac's lips twitched. Peterson must be all of eighteen years old.

"This is what we'll do," Browney started. "I'll place you where you should be. Cormac will be on your left. That's how you will know. Weren't you in the army?"

"We just shot straight ahead. I never knew what direction that was."

Heading north, Cormac exchanged greetings with fellow travelers. Where was Peterson from? Didn't everyone know which direction was which? People often got confused, but once a body knew where the north is, everything else became clear.

43

As the sky grew darker, he took care to avoid looking at any of the fires. It could affect his night vision. The area had many trees, notably the thorny mesquite. Good for firewood, but not for walking into.

A lot of animals were moving about, but he had grown accustomed to hearing those sounds. Tomorrow or the next day, they would be in the plains area. He needed to stock up on wood and put it in the back of the wagon. He should have done that anyway, just in case it rained.

As he searched for something to keep his mind occupied, thoughts of Brynn, the one person he didn't want to dwell on, crept in.

She had never socialized with people her own age. How odd. Not odd that it happened. It was peculiar that her father wanted it that way. Was he afraid she'd learn bad habits or influences? He sounded controlling, too controlling. He hadn't adequately prepared her for what would come after he passed away.

Waking up in the asylum must have been terrifying. The idea of being told you can't leave is beyond imagination. Well, he'd get their marriage annulled. She could have her freedom.

She was pretty and likable—

"Psst, O'Neill. It's me Peterson. Are you on my left only when I face the wagons? Like now you're on my right but if I turn around, you're on my left. I don't want to get this wrong."

If the situation wasn't so crucial, Peterson's bewildered expression would have been comical.

"When you face the circle, I'm on your left. If you turn and look outside the circle, I'm at your right. You'll just have to remember that. Where did you grow up?"

"New York City. I worked in a building, fixing looms all day. An enemy shot me and took me captive during the war.

I met my wife in the hospital. I had nothing to go back to, so I stayed in Texas. I want to build a brand-new life."

"Peterson? Are you out here?" Captain Browney whispered loudly.

"Go, just tell him you thought you heard something, but it was a deer."

"Gee, thanks O'Neill."

Cormac heard whispering, but it didn't sound like the captain was mad.

At midnight, Hugo Turner came and relieved him.

While returning to his wagon, he was taken aback when Brynn whispered to him.

"Everything fine?"

"Yes, goodnight."

He wished she had been waiting up for him, but she was likely guarding their wagon. She needed to learn how to shoot the rifle.

CHAPTER TEN

Four o'clock in the morning felt earlier on the trail than at her house. Keeping busy with work was something Brynn always enjoyed and had done a lot of. But this was going to take some getting used to. It felt difficult to wash, dress, cook breakfast, and load the wagon in less than an hour.

Once again, they had made the dough the night before. The coffee was ready to go. Cormac made sure the fire was nice and hot for cooking. Bacon didn't take long to cook.

After eating, they scrambled to get the wagon loaded. Usually Cormac helped, but he said something about needing wood for that evening. He acted like he knew what he was doing, so she didn't question him.

Daire gave her a quick lesson in loading, cocking, and aiming the rifle. Pulling the trigger was not part of the morning lesson.

"Brynn, if I have to tell you to sit down one more time, well I don't know what I'd do but you could be certain it would be something," Daire said, staring Brynn down.

Brynn laughed. "I'm not trying to vex you. We're running

out of time. Some of the wagons have lined up. Do you think they rise earlier than we do?" She furrowed her brow. "Maybe it was the rifle lesson."

"You got the quickest rifle lesson ever. I might ask some of the others later. They seem to know some trick to all this that we don't know. If we didn't eat, we could be first in line."

Cormac carried a load of wood to the back of the wagon and dumped it in. "Skipping meals isn't the answer. I have one more load of wood and we can go. Brynn, you ride up front with me. Those feet that I did not see need to heal."

Before she could protest, he was already in the forest.

"Good, your feet need a rest."

"Daire it's not fair that I ride."

Daire laughed. "Wait until we go over ruts and bumps. You'll be begging to walk. It's a necessity. *I* need your feet to heal. I'm not carrying you around if they get worse. We'll put new bandages and more of that sweet smelling concoction on when we stop for the noon meal."

"You're right about not wanting to carry me. But I just can't sit there all day."

Daire scrambled into the wagon from the front and came back out with a couple of dresses and a sewing basket. "It might be too bumpy but these need to be hemmed."

With a grateful smile, she accepted the bundle Daire held out to her.

The last of the wood had been placed in the back. Cormac walked toward her, and in an instant, he swept her off her feet. With her heart pounding, he gently seated her on the wagon's passenger side.

The temptation to call his actions unseemly beckoned to her, but she bit her lip to keep from speaking. The wagon jostled when Cormac climbed aboard. Without a word, he drove them to the line.

"We won't be the last. Looks like we'll be right in the

middle. Personally, I think it is the best position. If attacked from the front we have enough warning. Same thing if we are attacked from behind. I gave Daire a pistol to put in her pocket along with some bullets."

"We're riding into danger, aren't we?"

"The tribes along here are not happy with the treaties. They feel as though they were tricked. Plus, the number of buffalo is dwindling each year. To them we are interlopers. We stole their land and their food. I'd be angry too."

She nodded. Tribes? That meant more than one. A wave of shivers traveled up her spine.

Cormac glanced her way. "I didn't mean to scare you."

"I'm fine."

"Then why are you so pale all of a sudden?"

She bristled. "I most certainly am not."

Grinning, he glanced her way again. "You're right. Now you are a bright shade of red."

"Wagons ho!" The captain stood, waved his hat, and away they went.

As the wagon jerked forward, Brynn clung to the seat. Daire was probably right. It wouldn't be a relaxing ride doing nothing. Holding on was a struggle.

"TONIGHT, we'll make sure you know how to load and fire both the pistol and the rifle. If we are surrounded, you and Daire will help me keep my firearms loaded so I can continue shooting.

"That would be good to learn. Won't the sound of the gun alert the Indians that we are here?" Traveling wasn't the adventure she had thought it would be.

"They *know* we're here. Most likely we've been followed

the whole time. They don't always attack. Usually they want to trade."

Brynn furrowed her brow. "Trade what?"

"Any of the pretty women for safe passage."

She gasped, and he laughed.

"Cormac O'Neill you should be ashamed of yourself."

The grin on his face became broader. "No one has said my name that way except for my ma."

"Truthfully, do you really trade?"

"Yes. They like ribbons and goo gads. Sometimes they want food. A good wagon master worth his salt, packs extra for the trades. And Captain Browney is as good as it gets."

"I'm still uneasy about the whole thing. I might not sleep at night just thinking about it." She shook her head.

He studied her for a moment. "If you had fluttered your eyelashes, I would have assumed you were flirting with me. But your dropped jaw suggests you weren't flirting."

Quickly, she closed her mouth. Flirting? She didn't even know how. There seemed to be a plethora of things she didn't know. If only she was friendly like Daire or self-confident like Candace. Did her lack of knowledge make her boring? Why had he first perceived her words as flirting?

When she looked to her side of the wagon, she was astounded by the scenery. Earlier, they had been in a forest, but now all she could see was endless prairie grass.

"Is Daire getting through this tall grass easily?"

"Yes, she's following the trail from the people who are walking in front of her. Another reason the middle is a good place."

"I wish I hadn't gotten all those blisters. I should walk with her."

"It's not your fault. New shoes are stiff and unyielding. Plus, you walked a great distance. You need to stop being so hard on yourself. You're doing a fine job otherwise." His smile warmed her. "I'm glad you're here to be a friend for Daire."

Perhaps he was right about the shoes being stiff. As far as doing a great job, she *was* trying her best.

CHAPTER ELEVEN

*D*aire was approached by a little boy, who whispered something to her, and when she glanced at Cormac, terror was evident in her eyes.

"What's wrong?"

"Someone is looking for Brynn and me. She needs to get into the wagon and hide. I'd prefer to be sitting in front with you when they come. Hurry!"

Brynn wasted no time and swiftly dove into the wagon. Despite the tight squeeze, she managed to wriggle her way in. Cormac reached his hand down to Daire.

"Hold on, even if you think you are slipping. Remember I got you." He waited for her to nod and extend her hand.

Despite the moving wagon, he pulled her up, and she climbed over him to the passenger side.

"What are we going to do? I'm willing to wager that they know I played a role in helping Brynn escape and that you ended up marrying her." Daire's hands trembled.

"People are mistaken. Yes, you worked at the hospital. You know nothing about Mrs. Thistle."

"Cormac, people know her name is Brynn."

"You should take a moment to breathe deeply and calm down. Her name is Lynne. It rhymes with Brynn. She is indisposed," Cormac explained.

"She has diphtheria, and they shouldn't go near her," Daire added.

"That's a good one, Daire. Hold on, here they come." Cormac took a quick look over his shoulder. Good, he couldn't see Brynn; she must be well hidden.

Two men wearing gun belts, rode up.

Cormac scowled at them before disregarding their presence entirely.

"Hey, mister, I need you to stop this wagon," The man with the black hat demanded.

"No, I don't reckon so unless you're the law. You're not the law, are you?" Cormac yawned.

"We have a few questions for you and I'm assuming this is your wife?"

"This is my sister and no we are not stopping. In case you haven't noticed this is a wagon train. You don't stop."

"Hold on a moment!" the person wearing the brown hat declared, reaching for the wagon lines.

Cormac pulled his gun and cocked it. "I suggest you don't try that again," he growled.

"What in tarnation is going on here?" Captain Browney demanded.

"We have some questions for the O'Neills. Our sources confirm that this woman played a part in the escape of Mrs. Thistle from an asylum, and she is now married to this man," the older man explained.

"Makes no never mind to me. You can ask your questions when we stop in about four hours. Until then I kindly insist you ride drag."

"Mr. Thistle will not like that you kidnapped his wife," the man in black asserted.

"Rangers, are you? If you show me your badges, I'll halt the wagons," Captain Browney stated confidently, wearing a smile.

"We'll see you in about four hours," the man in black said. Both men turned their horses and rode toward the back of the line.

"Captain, if you want us to leave—"

"Absolutely not, Cormac. I fought in the war, same as most, but I didn't end up with a fancy horse or expensive clothes. They rub me the wrong way."

Captain Browney kept pace with Cormac's wagon.

"Now I don't want to get into your business, but I hope you have something to say to those two men when you stop."

Cormac nodded. "First, we're going to say Brynn is not the name of my wife. Her name is Lynne. Lynne Whistle, who is currently Lynne O'Neill. Daire worked at the hospital but does not know of Brynn. Plus, Brynn, er, that is, Lynne has diphtheria and won't be coming out of the wagon."

The captain tipped his hat. "Sounds like you have it all figured out. I'll have the soldiers on alert. Good luck." He rode off toward the front of the wagons.

WHY WOULDN'T her body stop shaking? Cormac's plan was a good one. All she had to do was rearrange the wagon and make a bed for herself. But what if they saw through the lies? What if they dragged her back to the asylum?

Tears slid down her face. Impatiently, she wiped them away. It had been a while since she'd last had a good cry, but now wasn't the right moment.

Would they believe she had diphtheria? Most likely she'd be on her way back to the asylum by evening. The Thistles were going too far. Wasn't committing her to the crazy hospital enough? After contemplating for what felt like an eternity, she had a potentially effective idea.

Quickly, she donned her night rail. She wasn't particularly inclined toward a bed cap, but she had seen one in a trunk. It required some effort to reorganize the wagon for her to access the trunk, but the outcome will be worthwhile. She hoped.

She pulled her hair back into a bun, using hair pins that belonged to Daire. Briefly, her heart sank. *Everything* belonged to her friend. There wasn't one item she could call her own. Sighing, she put on the cap and pulled hair here and there down from the bun to make it look like she'd been sleeping.

The next part was going to be painful, but a little agony would be worth it if her plan worked.

The wagons started to slow. The pit in her stomach grew. She drew a quilt over her and prayed.

Boisterous voices argued outside the wagon, and then it was quiet. The beating of her heart sounded particularly loud. If only she had a gun, not that she'd ever be able to shoot a person. What were they waiting for?

CHAPTER TWELVE

*C*ormac briefly squeezed Daire's hand. "It'll be fine," he whispered. He doubted he spoke the truth.

Taking his time, he descended and patiently watched as the two men and the captain dismounted from their horses. How had it come to this? His only goal was to bring his sister to the ranch, but it had unexpectedly become complicated.

The wagon's canvas billowed as the wind blew. "She's back here."

He untied the back of the canvas and opened it. "Lynne, how are you feeling?"

Looking inside, the two men gagged and quickly backed away.

"What is that smell?" The man in the black hat asked.

"Never mind the smell did you see all those sores on her feet. Is she covered in sores?" The other man asked.

"I told you she's been sick," Cormac reminded them.

"Now that you wasted our time, I bid you goodbye," Captain Browney said in disgust. He stared unwaveringly at the two men until they mounted their horses and made their exit.

Cormac let out the breath he'd been holding. What a relief.

"Daire? I need your help," Brynn called out.

Captain Browney took off his hat and then shook his head. "How sick is she and is it contagious?" A tinge of resignation could be heard in his voice.

"She has blisters on her feet and Mrs. Harris gave her a jar of some foul-smelling stuff to rub on them. Cormac grinned.

Captain Browney chuckled. "If that don't beat all! There's bound to be a lot of questions. I'm hoping to hear the true story soon. I'd like to know what we're dealing with." He arched his right brow. "You didn't marry a married woman, did you?"

"Of course not. We haven't done anything illegal. I doubt they'll be back. Even if they suspect we were lying, they'll probably figure her for dead. It's not my story to tell, but I'm sure Brynn will tell you soon enough."

"Grab some food, we'll be leaving shortly." The captain took his horse's reins and led him away.

"Is he gone?" Daire asked from the back of the wagon.

"Yes, and we have a bunch of spectators. We should eat. The captain said we'd be leaving again soon."

"I'll finish bandaging Brynn's feet and get you your noon meal. Brynn will be getting dressed, so it's best to stay away from the wagon for a little while."

"Just hand me the coffee pot and a cup. I'll be fine." It was a tip he'd learned in the Army. Always make two pots of coffee each morning. The second pot lasted most of the day. Lukewarm coffee was still coffee. Retrieving the items from Daire, he found a spot on the ground and leaned against the front wheel. He poured the coffee and sighed deeply after the first sip. It had been a long morning. The plan had worked well with all Brynn's efforts to make it real. His nerves of steel slipped a bit. No matter which way he examined the situation, he couldn't come up with anything else to do. The possibility of having to let her go had been humbling.

———

STRING BEANS, her legs felt like string beans. How could she be standing? After taking a step, she grabbed onto the side of the wagon. Her feet hurt, and weakness shrouded her.

Luckily, Cormac stood up and wrapped his arm around her waist. "It's going to be fine. Why don't we sit for a while? You don't look so good." He supported her as she settled on the ground and propped her against the back wheel.

Walking toward the front wooden wheel, he retrieved his coffee and cup before joining her. "That was stressful. You did a remarkable job with the concoction on your blisters."

"It surely made them flee, didn't it?" She tried to laugh, but it didn't happen. With unsteady hands, she accepted the cup Cormac offered. "I must admit I was so scared. The Thistles have no claim on me, but they do have money. More so now if they are using my funds. They can have every cent. I'd rather be free of them. But I must acknowledge that this whole thing leaves a bitter taste in my mouth."

"It was a tense moment for sure. I wasn't sure what would happen. Do they have a phony marriage certificate? We haven't been traveling with this group long enough to know whether they'd have our back."

His hand brushed against the back of hers. It gave her a sense of comfort. Why, though? It was just a hand touching hers.

Daire climbed out of the wagon carrying a basket. "We've got biscuits, preserves, and bacon. This should hold us over. I've put together a few biscuits with bacon and wrapped them. This way, if you or Brynn get hungry during the trip you'll be able to easily reach into the wagon and retrieve them."

"What about you?" Brynn asked.

Daire patted her pocket. "I have a pocketful, and I fashioned a jug with a cord so I can carry water with me."

Cormac grinned. "You're certainly inventive."

"Not really, I just observed what others did. Looks like everyone is getting set to roll out." Standing, she dusted off any crumbs from her dress and carefully placed her poke bonnet back on her head.

Brynn began to stand but was immediately swept off her feet and positioned on the front wagon bench. This time, it didn't startle her as it usually did when Cormac lifted her up. He handed her the basket, which she placed right behind them.

Scaling the wagon, he settled beside her and offered a full canteen.

"Should I put this in the back too?"

"Let's leave it resting at our feet. I couldn't locate it readily earlier today when it was in the back. As hot as it's been I don't think putting it in back will keep it any cooler."

"Wagons ho!" the captain shouted, which really meant everyone should wait their turn while all the wagons in front of them began moving.

Brynn frowned.

"Are you all right?"

"Just impatient, I suppose. I want as much distance between me and those men. I wonder what Mrs. Thistle will say when they return empty handed."

"I've been wondering that too. Maybe she'll see through the Brynn-Lynn ruse, since you're traveling with Daire. I mean they seemed to know Daire helped you escape. There's also the fact that I told them you are my wife, but I can't be certain that will be taken as truth." He stared into the distance briefly. Then he smiled. "However, your performance was exceptional. I know you didn't wish for me to see your feet, but I have to say they look bad. And the smell... horrid. It made their eyes water. But you also managed to look out of sorts. The sleeping cap was a great addition."

Heat infused her whole body. Dealing with compliments was challenging. If only she possessed some social etiquette, she could rely upon.

"I'm glad it worked. It broke my heart to think I'd have to leave Daire and you. You two have been more of a family to me than any I've ever had. I was an only child. You two are blessed to have each other."

"You have us now." He flicked the lines, and they started off.

This time, she didn't make the effort to bring the dresses up front with her. It was too bumpy to sew the hems."

"It's pretty country," she said, breaking the easy silence that had fallen between them. "I've never come across places with such a vast amount of grass. It's soothing to watch the switchgrass flowing with the wind. What's it like where your ranch is?"

"We have open spaces too, but there are plenty of trees. It's a great place to run a ranch. The Trinity River is about five miles away. We initially decided to make our home by the river, but the flies and mosquitoes were unbearable. I'm used to being outside, but the pests were the worst I'd ever experienced. There was just no way to escape them. I felt bad for the homesteaders who settled in the colder weather and didn't realize just how bad it was until winter was over. Luckily, we didn't make a claim on any property there. Some simply couldn't afford to buy more land."

"That's awful! It sounds as though there were swarms everywhere!"

"Yes, there were. Devlin and I both have 320 acres

combined. We received 160 each for the Homestead Act. It's a large piece of property. There's plenty of grass and water. Room for building a house for each. Right now, we only have one house. We have a good-sized barn too. Rounding up cattle has been relatively easy enough, and our herd has been increasing." His words echoed with a strong sense of pride.

"I can't wait to see it," she said softly.

CHAPTER THIRTEEN

"Circle up!" A loud cry went up among the travelers.

"What's going on?" Brynn asked, her voice shrill.

Cormac slowed and reached his hand out to catch his sister's. He grabbed her arm instead. She gasped as he pulled her into the wagon, but he didn't have a choice. Something was wrong. Very wrong.

Daire was precariously balanced, trying to sit on the bench next to him as fear danced in her eyes. "What—"

Cormac grabbed the extra rifle. Daire, I need you to move into the wagon. Take the rifle and cover the back. Keep your head down. I have a bad feeling." As soon as his sister climbed into the back, she reached out and took the rifle.

"I'll grab more bullets. Do you have enough?"

"Yes! Just get down. Brynn, I want you in the back too."

Amid the chaos, Cormac firmly held onto the lines, determined to keep the horses in check.

"Circle! Circle!"

"I can't release my grip long enough to get in the back!" She sounded like she was on the brink of hysteria.

"Brynn, get down on the floor!" he commanded.

The wagon veered, and Cormac pulled the horses to a stop. He quickly tied off the lines. Grabbing the rifle, he jumped down and reached up for Brynn. After he lifted her down, he called to his sister. "Climb out the front. It's safer." Holding his breath, he anxiously awaited Daire's arrival. He quickly swung her down.

"Under the wagon behind the wheels!"

He reached under the seat and grabbed all the bullets he could carry, plus two loaded pistols. Kneeling on one knee, he peered around the circle. The commotion was so loud it was hard to tell what was happening. Whoever was attacking them had guns and arrows.

A man took an arrow and fell to the ground. One glance at the arrow and he instantly knew they were being attacked by Comanche Indians.

Daire was suddenly shooting, and he dived under the wagon and pulled his rifle up, ready to shoot. There were so many of them, most on horses. The Comanche were a fierce tribe. He'd gone up against a few in his time, but nothing like this.

Suddenly, they screamed and rode off, brandishing their rifles in the air as if in celebration.

"You two all right?" he yelled as he scooted toward the two women.

"We're not hurt," Daire told him.

"I'm going to find out what that was all about. Stay here."

"Don't leave," Daire pleaded.

"Hold on, I'll return soon," he murmured while creeping through the grass, examining the area within the circle. Only the one man seemed to have been injured. Cormac stood, and by the time he reached the wounded man, there was a big crowd gathering.

"Back to your wagons and stand guard!" Captain

Browney called. "Get back! Idiot greenhorn almost got us killed. No one shoots buffalo! Got it?"

Cormac blinked in surprise. Everyone knew not to shoot buffalo. Their numbers were dwindling, and the Indians were fierce about protecting what was left. Walking back to his wagon, he was filled with anger. His family could have gotten killed all over a buffalo.

Brynn stood. "What happened?"

"Didn't I explicitly say to both of you to stay beneath the wagon?"

The moment he saw the hurt on her face, he regretted his words. "Why don't we take a moment to sit down? I need to calm down and catch my breath."

Brynn and Daire exchanged glances and then sat staring at him expectantly.

"Those were the Comanche. It seems that someone thought it was fine to kill a buffalo."

Daire gasped. "Why would anyone do that?"

"Some of the people we're traveling with are inexperienced. Apparently, not everyone in Texas understands the importance of staying away from buffalo. We could have been killed."

"Brynn?" Cormac slid next to her and pulled her into his arms. Her eyes were filled with tears, and she looked incredibly forlorn.

"You must think me such a baby."

"No, of course not. This type of violence wasn't part of your upbringing. I was shaking too," he attempted to reassure her.

HER BODY CONTINUED TO SHAKE, despite the comfort of his

warm embrace. "I'm sorry, I'm trying to calm down. It doesn't seem to be working."

"Daire and I grew up on a ranch. We've been confronted by Indians before. Not that it's ever easy. It's just not as shocking 'to us as it is to you. Did you live anywhere else besides San Antonio?"

Inhaling deeply, she let it out slowly. "We lived in Georgia when I was very young. I only remember the house in San Antonio. The only danger I had to fight was a mouse with a broom. I did manage to sweep it out of the house. It might be a while before I'm comfortable with gun fights."

He smiled. "I'm not sure you every get comfortable but it does take some experience with such things before you know what to do. The confusion intensifies the panic."

Her sense of safety grew as she found solace in his embrace. His arms had been around her far too long. Slowly, she edged away.

"Folks! We still have a ways to go! Get ready to line up!" Captain Browney shouted out.

"I suppose it's not a good idea to stay here," Brynn stated as she stood up and brushed the dirt off her dress.

"At least we didn't unpack anything," Daire commented. "Brynn how are your feet?"

"The same. I would have thought they'd have been healed by now, but I suppose it takes time." As she moved toward the front of the wagon, Cormac lifted her onto it once again. She took a seat and grimaced in pain. How does he tolerate sitting on the hard bench day after day? A cushion would do a world of good right now.

He climbed up and gave her a long look. "Are you sure you're fine?"

She mustered a smile and acknowledged with a nod. "You endure things because you have to. I'm still quaking, but I'll manage. Don't worry about me, we don't want to be last in line."

With a chuckle, he grabbed the lines and released the brake. "Daire ready?"

"Let's get going," she called up to him.

Hours passed as they journeyed through the tall grass, occasionally encountering rolling hills and then flat land once again.

"There should be a few streams up ahead. If we're lucky we'll stop near one," he commented.

"I'd like to wash up properly," she said before she realized it was unseemly to talk about such things with a man. Her face heated.

Cormac laughed. "Unseemly?"

"You could say that."

"At least it wasn't me this time."

She couldn't resist grinning back as his infectious grin spread. Rarely had she smiled while at home. It was a freeing feeling; one she was starting to enjoy, even long for.

Cormac was so intent on driving, she was able to sneak a glance at him unawares. He was a handsome man with chiseled features. A strong chin with a beard that has been growing for a couple of days on it. His dark hair was hardly seen under his hat, but she knew it was dark and wavey and he often pushed it back with his fingers.

His skin had a deep complexion from the sun. She must look pale beside him. He probably spent his days in the sun. His gray eyes were filled with a great deal of expression. She could gauge his mood by looking into his eyes. Often, they held humor and compassion. His grin was boyish and endearing.

Her breath caught. Endearing? She swiftly shifted her gaze to the wagon in front of her. Stop staring at Cormac or dwelling on his appearance. It wouldn't do. He possibly had a woman he wanted to marry close to his ranch. There were too many things she didn't ask.

Selfish, that was the proper word for her. She needed help, and the O'Neills had offered it to her. They had their own lives and plans before she was inserted into their lives. It would be best if she kept her distance from Cormac at least.

She hadn't considered it before, but when those men came for her, they all could have been removed from the wagon train. She burdened them like a millstone. Until her feet healed, she was powerless, but she would make certain they would not regret bringing her along.

"Good, I see the stream up ahead. It's good sized too. We'll be stopping soon."

"Rest assured, once I'm fully healed, I'll make sure to carry my load and then some. I feel like a leech."

He gazed into her eyes. "Never that." He turned his attention back to driving.

For once, she had no idea what he meant. She had no understanding of what the look in his eyes meant either.

CHAPTER FOURTEEN

*T*he wonderful sensation of the cool water on her legs and feet, coupled with the sound of women laughing, brought her joy.

Daire laughed along with the others, and soon Brynn joined in. It had been challenging to know if people wanted to be her friend or if they only wanted to gossip about her. She'd heard her name whispered more than once, and it had stunned and saddened her.

Daire had counseled her to just be herself, but it was hard when she didn't even know who she was. Everyone else had lives, families, and hopes for their future. Brynn had none of these things. What was she to say to these women?

"How's married life?" Bea Turner asked her.

Brynn turned toward the rounded woman and smiled. Bea stiffened, clearly astonished. Then she gave a nod.

"It's been fine," answered Brynn. "How are you and your husband, Hugo isn't it?" she asked politely.

"We're as happy as two peas in a pod. We have a homestead waiting for us along the Trinity River. The house and barn are already built. We didn't have to pay a thing for it, neither. My Hugo is a smart man. You haven't had a chance for alone time with your man, have you?"

In surprise, Brynn drew in a breath. "Excuse me?"

"I'm just saying that a fine man like Cormac can have any woman he wants. He's been spending a lot of time in the woods lately. Does he go alone?" A slow smile crept over Bea's face, and she gazed intently at Brynn as though she was waiting for a reaction.

"Your husband doesn't go into the woods?" she asked.

From the merriment in Bea's eyes, she realized she had fallen into her trap.

"Hugo goes in, but it doesn't take him long. I know where he is always, especially during guard duty when lonely women come and keep the men company."

"That's good. It was nice talking with you," Brynn called over her shoulder as she scrambled up the bank.

Which was it? Was it in the woods or during guard duty that Bea was insinuating Cormac was up to no good?

Bea was probably discussing it right now.

Daire chased after her, and they walked to their wagon together.

"Don't listen to Bea. She's just trying to make trouble." Daire took Brynn's hand and gave it a quick squeeze before she let it drop.

"I know. I just don't like to be her topic of conversation is all."

"Perfectly understandable. Let's get those feet dried and then prepare supper. We're staying here an extra day so the men can hunt. It will be nice to have a change of menu."

Brynn nodded when she was supposed to, but getting Bea's words off her mind felt like an insurmountable task. What did it all mean? Asking Daire would only lead to embarrassment.

She turned toward the sound of the group cheering.

Many of the men were back with venison, plenty for them all. Sebastion Peterson brought their portion to them. Both women thanked him profusely until he turned a bright shade of red.

"Cormac told me to tell you he'll be back in a while," Sebastion informed them.

"Did he say why?" Brynn asked, frowning in confusion.

"Not really, he just said he had things to do. I'd best get back to my wife." He skedaddled away.

"What's Cormac up to?"

Daire lifted her shoulders. "Who knows?"

Brynn busied herself by dicing the meat into fine cubes. They added dried peas to soak with the beans from the night before. Hopefully, the meal would be pleasant.

"I could mix up some cornmeal for Johnnycakes," Daire offered.

"Great idea. I just wish I could help more."

Daire patted her shoulder. "Don't you worry one minute about it. Besides, once you're healed, I expect you to run circles around me."

"I will. It's a promise."

THE SUN HAD SET about an hour earlier. Everyone at the camp was busy cooking, and the aroma was pleasing. Cormac nodded to a few people on his way back to his wagon. A cozy sight greeted him. Daire's face was animated while she talked to Brynn, who was laughing.

It was pleasant to have someone besides his partner Devlin to come home to. He ran his fingers through his wet hair and placed his hat once again on his head. It felt great to be clean. He didn't always have a chance to shave, but he didn't take pleasure in having a beard.

"Did you save me any?" he asked.

"As a matter of fact, we were just wondering if we should eat your share," Daire joked.

"You didn't want any Johnnycakes did you?" Brynn teased.

"You two are incorrigible. I'm mighty hungry, and yes, I would like a Johnnycake or two." He smiled. After grabbing his plate and fork, he helped himself to supper. He chewed his first forkful and swallowed. "This is good."

"You can thank Daire. It was all her doing. I'm a lady of leisure these days," Brynn told him in a wry tone.

"Thank you, Daire, it's a fine supper."

"Sebastion delivered our portion and mentioned you'd be a while, but he didn't know why," Brynn shared before she glanced away.

Did she care? Had she been worried about him? Curious? She sure was a puzzle.

"Looking as good as me is a process that takes time."

"I knew there was something different about you. You finally bathed. My, it's been so long I forgot what you really looked like," Daire teased.

"It was a nice treat. Tomorrow, I'll take you upstream and you two can bathe." He smiled at Brynn's startled expression. "Don't worry I won't look. Upstream the water is cleaner. I'll stand guard with my back turned, promise."

His lips twitched as he watched her expression change from outrage to confusion to whatever it was now. She was in deep thought, he knew, but what was she dwelling on?

COULD SHE FEEL MORE AWKWARD? Cormac trailed behind. It shouldn't make her nervous after all. Daire was his sister and

Cormac was trustworthy. It existed solely in her mind, yet her heart refused to stop pounding.

Tempted to go back twice, she didn't want to look foolish, at least not that morning.

They had passed many of the others on their trip upstream. Most were friendly except Bea, who told Daire she wasn't needed to help the newlyweds. It was dig after dig with Bea. What was her problem? What was she trying to suggest?

Her foot collided with a protruding tree root, and Daire luckily reached out and steadied her in time. Well, now she didn't have to worry about looking ridiculous. It could have been worse. She could have fallen headfirst onto the dirt.

They found themselves in a delightful spot, surrounded by trees that offered shade. Best of all, it was deserted.

"Are you positive no one can see?" Brynn asked.

"I'm standing guard. Just go in with whatever it is you wear under those dresses and have at it. I'll sit here with my back to you. Take your time. If anyone shows up, I'll let you know. You can just duck into the water until they are gone."

"Come on Brynn. It'll be fun," Daire cajoled.

Brynn quickly pulled her dress over her head and edged into the cool water. The bottom was a bit rocky, but once she got toward the middle, she didn't need to stand on her feet, as the water was deeper.

"I wasn't sure you knew how to swim," Daire commented as she stood in a shallower spot and rubbed the soap through her hair.

"There was a river not too far from the house. My friend Allison, the cook, taught me. I was never allowed to be gone long, but once we ran down to the river." Brynn swam to where Daire stood and took the soap that was given to her. She didn't add that Allison was fired for going with her.

"This soap smells so good! I was unaware that soap could

have such a scent! In fact, I had to make our soap, and it didn't smell like this."

"It was a present from my brother. He can be very sweet and charming at times."

"I can hear you," Cormac called out. "Brynn, this is where you confirm that he is sweet, charming, and handsome." He laughed.

"I was brought up to never tell a lie," she shot back. She smiled when Cormac's laugh grew louder.

Daire giggled as she took the soap and washed herself. She handed it back to Brynn to do the same.

"I know no one is here now, but a person could approach at any time," Daire said.

"I was thinking the same thing. Let's get out." Brynn winced as she walked across the rocks. Grabbing a towel, she dried her face, hands, and feet before she sat on it. She grabbed her dress, quickly pulled it over her head and smoothed it down. They would change into clean clothes when they returned to the wagon.

The women put on their hose and shoes before allowing Cormac to turn back around.

"That didn't take long," he commented.

"I was thinking we probably should try to wash some clothes since we're already wet," Brynn suggested.

"I was thinking the same," Daire agreed.

They returned to the wagon and gathered up the dirty clothes and this time they brought lye soap with them. There were numerous women at the edge of the stream washing clothes.

CHAPTER FIFTEEN

*D*espite the scorching sun, standing in the stream provided relief from the heat. Some women had more than one pile of clothes to wash. They were all bent over, scrubbing the clothes and soon all the women had their hands on the small of their backs.

Despite the toil, the women were a cheery lot. Many shared their wishes and dreams of where they aimed to settle. A few had amusing stories about their children. The time went quickly and before she knew it, they were done. A lack of clothing plus having the two of them hurried them along.

At least no one asked her how married life was. She didn't have an answer to that question. She was overcome with sadness, but she quickly brushed it aside. This was only temporary. She paid attention to where the best places were to settle. She'd need to find a place for herself, eventually.

Cormac set up a line for them to hang the clean clothes to let them dry. He certainly was thoughtful.

From the other side of the wagon, a female voice could be heard. "When I get married, I want a husband like you."

"I'm certain that once your family finds a place to settle, you'll have no shortage of potential suitors," Cormac replied.

"I wish we were—"

"I bet your family is looking for you," Cormac interrupted.

Brynn's heart plummeted. Was this what Bea had been hinting about?

Daire shook her head and hurried to the other side of the wagon. "Cormac, who was that?"

"The Belden girl. She comes over from time to time, and I always send her home. I don't want an angry father coming after me. I might need to talk to him about the situation. She follows me around, and it certainly doesn't look right."

Brynn wished she could chase after this girl, but she really didn't have any claim on Cormac. The entire thing caused her stomach to churn. If Cormac was free, maybe he'd prefer the girl. She followed him around? Into the woods?

She climbed into the wagon and changed into clean clothes. It wasn't her business, and she'd best remember that fact or she'd have a massive heartbreak. She sat inside the wagon. Where were these thoughts coming from? Where were these feelings coming from?

Taking a few shaky breaths, she released the air slowly, attempting to soothe her nerves. What was wrong with her? She'd always prided herself on being level-headed. This wouldn't do at all. She wanted a simple orderly life, and that was what she aimed to achieve.

LUCKILY, Daire accompanied him to gather firewood. He wanted to be sure to gather extra. They might be surrounded by trees now, but there was another stretch of grassland ahead.

"I haven't encouraged her," he blurted.

"I'm aware of that, Cormac. Maybe you *should* have a talk with her father. Bea Turner keeps hinting you are in the woods for a considerable amount of time, and she hinted that you've had a visitor during guard duty. She said these things to Brynn to provoke her, but Brynn didn't react."

He sighed. "I'll figure something out." Bea would be right. Beth Beldon wasn't the sweet girl she pretended to be. He'd never known such a forward female. He walked to the other side of the camp. Brynn was on her feet cooking. A smile tugged at his lips. He had an idea.

"Brynn how would feel about walking out with me after supper?" It took all his effort not to laugh or grin at her surprise.

"Should I feel a certain way about it?" Her brow furrowed.

"I would regard it as a tremendous favor."

She tilted her head and gazed at him.

"It appears that Beth Belden has feelings for me, but I need her to direct her attention elsewhere. She knows we're married. I've explained it often enough, but she won't stop following me. I thought perhaps if we walked around the camp together, she'd understand the notion of finding another beau."

"Another beau?" She placed the ladle she had been using to stir the stew onto a plate. Then she faced him. She took a deep breath.

This was not going to bode well for him. He smiled.

"Why would she view you as a beau? You must have done something to encourage her. Maybe you smiled at her or you tried to stand next to her at a meeting we had. Maybe—"

"Brynn, please lower your voice. I have never encouraged anyone, including you.

By her expression, it was evident he'd said the wrong thing.

"What I mean is she just started following me." He lifted his left shoulder and let it drop.

Brynn's eyes narrowed. "I know I have no claim on you, and I never will, but don't humiliate me in front of all these people. I don't think I could take it. It's only a couple of weeks and you'll be done with me. It'll be as if I was never in your life." With her arms folded, she briefly focused on the ground, then looked up and made eye contact with him. "Of course I'll walk with you. One good turn deserves another."

One good turn? Oh boy. "I need to gather more wood." He started to walk away when he heard her.

"Of course you do."

What had he done, exactly? He wasn't about to allow a woman to control his life. He'd witnessed enough between his partner Devlin and his former girlfriend to know it wasn't for him. No harpy for him. To think he'd thought Brynn to be nice, kind, generous even. There was no denying how pretty... No, she was a harpy, and that was that.

He grabbed as much wood as he could carry. Imagining Brynn's face if he came back empty-handed soured him, but then he laughed. The whole thing was ridiculous. It had stung when she'd declared she was done with him at the end of the trail. He didn't like it one bit.

"FOR HEAVEN'S SAKE! You two appear as if you're ready for a funeral," Daire said.

"It's him."

"It's her." They both spoke at the same time.

"I'm not pleased with either of you. I refuse to be thrown off this train because of the two of you. Now act in love."

They looked at each other.

"Now."

Brynn nodded. It wasn't worth getting Daire so exasperated. It certainly wasn't how a friend acted.

Cormac reached out his hand, and she grasped it. They headed for the outside circle of the wagons. His hand's warmth filled her with confidence.

"For Daire's sake," she whispered.

"Yes, for Daire. I don't want to sound critical, but your fake smile doesn't appear genuine."

"It's not supposed to look good. It's fake." She chuckled. It was a relief when he joined in. Suddenly, they relaxed a bit and began their walk.

"Are we supposed to be talking about anything? While we stroll, I mean." She glanced at him.

"I think talking is better than if we smile."

She squeezed his hand, hard. He gasped ever so softly, and her real smile returned.

"It brings you joy to witness my suffering. Good to know. Seriously though, I didn't encourage Beth. If you take a quick look at her father's wagon you can witness her fawning all over that soldier.

"His name is Jim."

"You know the soldiers, do you? Interesting." He lightly squeezed her hand.

"Ouch! It brings you joy to witness my suffering? Good to know. Besides, I know mostly everyone's name." Her smile grew wider as his lips twitched.

"I barely squeezed your hand."

"I'm a delicate butterfly." She couldn't help it. She laughed.

"Indeed, you are, my little cherub." There was merriment in his voice.

"I've been called worse." Her laughter faded. "I'm sorry, we're enjoying ourselves and I think of things better left alone."

"I think we all have things like that."

They'd made it about three quarters of the way when Beth's parents stepped out from the shadows and into their path.

CHAPTER SIXTEEN

"Good evening," Cormac greeted.

"This isn't that kind of visit," Milo Belden barked.

"It's about our daughter Beth," his wife, Freya explained.

Cormac let go of Brynn's hand and drew her close, grateful she allowed him to put his arm around her waist.

"There's been talk about you and her. O'Neill, you'd best explain yourself."

"It's not my husband's fault," Brynn defended. "I've watched your daughter, and though she tends to stand too close to people she seems fine. My husband made it clear today that she needed to stay far away. You see people are beginning to make assumptions and we don't want anything to smudge Beth's reputation."

Cormac stiffened. He had never experienced a woman defending him before. He was torn between liking it and being irritated.

Freya sighed. "Thank you for looking out for her. I didn't want to believe Bea. I know you are newly married. But Bea kept insisting. Now that I think about it, she says a lot of things about many people. Come on, Milo. Let's let these two love birds continue their walk."

Milo tipped his hat and followed his wife into the inner circle.

"I'm sorry." Brynn gazed up at him. "I probably shouldn't have said anything. I'm unsure about when it's appropriate for me to speak up. My father did all the talking. Then Mrs. Thistle after that. I'm just as shocked as you are that I spoke up."

Cormac pulled her closer for a quick hug. "You can be my little love bird anytime."

She turned a becoming shade of crimson before she stepped away from him.

"I did just wash in the stream," he reminded her.

"I'm not quite sure what to do with you. It's fun to banter with you. When you tease me about love, I have no idea what to say back. My face starts to burn, and I wish I could vanish."

"I wouldn't want to be the cause of you vanishing. I'll try to be considerate when I speak to you, though I make no promises. Sometimes things come out before I can stop them. I guess we're back to cherub?"

She laughed. "I need a name for you."

"There's always honey, sweetheart, sugarplum. I'm sure I can think of many if I put my mind to it."

"Sugarplum, I like that one. I bet you like it too or you wouldn't have suggested it."

"I see you trying not to laugh at me. No rough, tough rugged cowboy is called sugarplum. How about Most Honored One? King of the Castle?"

"I suspected you were a bit touched in the head, but now I know for sure, sugarplum." She put her hands on her hips and stared at him.

She was a spitfire for certain. It was good she'd gained

some confidence from when he'd first met her. "I think Daire will be wondering where we are." He reached out for her and smiled when she put her tiny hand in his.

"Daire is a smart girl. She knows where the circle outside of the wagons is. If she needed us, she'd find us," Brynn said.

"Hmm."

"What's that supposed to mean?" she asked.

He began walking and waited a minute before answering her. "If I say anything, you have a reason why I'm wrong. Have you been hiding this stubborn streak you possess?"

She opened her mouth twice, but nothing came out. Finally, she slowed her walk. "I'm not stubborn. I had it beat out of me long ago. It's an undesirable trait in a young lady."

"Your father beat you?"

She nodded. "Didn't yours?"

"No."

She came to a stop. "Now you're fibbing. All children must be beaten into submission. I've heard our pastor say it on more than one occasion."

With his hands on her shoulders, he turned her until they were face to face. "Not all fathers beat their children. Children can be raised with love and guidance."

The way her eyes widened touched his heart. Her childhood must have been horrific.

"I thought— Then why?" Tears filled her eyes.

"Hey, now. Let's not talk about such sad things, my love bird cherub." His heart lit up at her tentative smile.

"I'll be fine, sugarplum. We'd best get back."

"Good idea." Once again, he held her hand all the way to their wagon.

Daire smiled. "Well, it's about time. You two must be the slowest walkers ever."

Brynn smiled at him, and he gladly smiled back.

"FOLKS, I know it's Sunday, but I need us to get a move on. There's a herd of cattle coming behind us, and on the Chisholm Trail, cattle drives take precedence. If we stay here, we'll be here at least another day. The cattle will need to be watered and rested while we wait for our turn to start out. I'm not of the mind to eat dust riding behind cattle if it can be helped," Captain Browney announced.

Most of the people went back to their wagons to pack up, but a good many insisted on church services. They planned to stay behind.

"What's going to happen to those who refuse to roll out with the rest of us?" Daire asked.

"They will be separated from us for a while. The cattle could end up between us as we travel," Cormac surmised.

"That wouldn't be safe, would it?" Brynn asked?

"I wouldn't think so," Cormac answered. "Most folks will pray and read the Bible at some point today."

"God would understand surely," Daire said.

Brynn nodded. "God is with us everywhere we go. He is all around us. But people need to make their own decisions. Sunday is God's day. But we do need to keep moving. During the war there were times when we missed services. We didn't dare go outside if Union Soldiers were there. My father said there is always an exception."

She put the last of the cookware into a wooden box already set in the back of the wagon. Scanning the area, she made sure they hadn't forgotten anything.

"Brynn, I'll help you up," Cormac offered.

"That's nice of you but I'm walking today, at least for a while."

Cormac stared at her. She stared back until he nodded. Then she hooked elbows with Daire and began to walk.

"You and my brother are getting along," Daire commented.

"We always got along," Brynn said.

"You seem closer since your walk. It's none of my business."

"Daire you're my best friend. Of course it's your business. We were met by Beth's parents, Freya and Milo. I told them I had been there when Beth came around. I did say that Cormac has discouraged Beth and that we were growing concerned about her reputation."

"What did they say?"

"They were grateful since there had been some talk. I believe Bea's name was mentioned. The Beldens plan to keep a better eye on her. I hope they do. Beth was talking to one of the soldiers last evening."

"I'm glad that's over. I know you were tired of Bea's comments as was I. How many people do you think stayed behind?"

"I think I saw five wagons not joining us. All we can do is pray they stay safe. Maybe they'll be able to join up with us this evening or tomorrow. Prayer is a powerful thing. Miracles happen every day."

"I agree."

CHAPTER SEVENTEEN

*T*he feeling of cold water on Brynn's feet was absolutely wonderful. Not until after they finished eating and completed all their tasks did she bring up the subject of her feet. Pulling her weight was essential.

With a tender tone, Cormac chided, "You should have spoken up."

"You yourself said I was stubborn. I guess I am. Besides it's not like last time. This is mainly a soak and then bandage so I can walk tomorrow. Preventative, I guess you could say." She took a deep breath.

Cormac had been by her side ever since she put her feet in the basin of water. Before finally dozing off last night, she'd made a promise to herself to avoid Cormac. Nothing positive could come of them being playful or whatever it was called. Certainly not flirting or being too forward? In fact, she didn't know what it was about. It involved talking to a man. Her spine tingled with a cold shudder.

Was it true that not all fathers were so strict with their children? It's possible that not all of them were, but most were probably strict. No one in school had ever said a thing about it. Every aspect of her life revolved around not upsetting her father, but she'd thought…

"You all right?" Cormac asked. "You were just making the strangest of faces."

Without glancing at him, she nodded. "I'm fine."

"Are you sure?" His intent gaze added to her discomfort.

She knew how to behave politely and speak respectfully, especially toward the widows she'd been around, but this situation was unique. Things were immensely different from when her father was alive. She was now in uncharted territory, but certainly politeness and respect were still expected. It was the aspects of friendship and being around Cormac too often that made her falter. Walking instead of riding was supposed to put a distance between them. But she was wrong. In truth, she had no clue about what she was doing.

"Honestly, I'm unsure how to navigate our friendship or define our relationship. I don't know how to make conversation with people. I've always been in the background of life. With you, I'm right there in front. I don't want to lead you on, or whatever it's referred to. Mrs. Thistle accused me of trifling with men. I was filled with shame at my unintentional behavior. That played a role in my decision to get engaged. I needed to stop her from accusing me of being a hussy or anything else she believed I was.

"I did receive many bouquets of flowers from gentlemen callers. But it didn't turn my head. I'm aware I am a spinster, and they just wanted my inheritance. None of my suitors ever gave me a compliment. I guess that's what you would call them, suitors.

"When this journey is over, you'll be grateful to be free from me. I can run a household. I can clean and do any chore there is. Well, I don't know all the chores involved with ranch life, but I'm sure I could tackle them. It's the fact that

I'm socially inept that renders me not suitable. Maybe I can find a widower who wouldn't care I'm a plain spinster."

"Can you cook? I know you can cook beans and camp food but what about a pie?" He smiled.

"My father insisted that my cooking was inedible. I never had an opportunity to bake a pie but I'm sure it wouldn't be editable."

"That does pose a problem. Maybe you just lack experience and the right teacher? In the western regions, the notion of being a spinster doesn't hold true. The number of men is greater than the number of women. A widower might have children of his own. It's possible that he'll be significantly older. Are you seeking a man with wealth?"

She gaped at him. "You're teasing me. I believe I won't be the one making the decision. If somebody will have me..."

"That's what it takes? You could have your choice. Although you may encounter gunslingers and outlaws, I'm confident you'll find a suitable person. Could be a farmer or a store owner. Did you have your heart set on living in town?"

"I'd like to imagine it would be someone I could love. In the end I'm sure with God's guidance I will find the right man. What about you? Do you have a person in mind to marry?" Her chest expanded with the breath she held. She slowly let it out, waiting for him to answer.

"I haven't had much time to acquaint myself with any of the women in town. I did attend church a few times but as soon as the service was over, I had to hightail it out of there. I had several mothers eager to introduce their daughters to me." A grin spread across his face.

"Really? Did any attract your interest? I mean there must have been a few pretty candidates."

"Devlin and I were too preoccupied with our escape to spare a moment to look. Besides, you can't determine by what a woman wears to church if she's suited to ranch life. Nice dresses aren't needed except for church."

"You do have a point I suppose. I arrived in an asylum gown. I must be on one of your lists now."

"List?"

She nodded. "You know, appropriate or not appropriate. Perhaps sane or insane?"

"Where do you come up with these ideas?" He laughed.

She joined in, and it felt like pure heaven.

"I'm going to dry and bandage my feet now…"

He stood. "I know, I know it would be unseemly if I stay." He smiled and walked toward the middle of the circle where other men had already gathered.

A WIDOWER? A man who wouldn't have any objections to marrying a spinster? Did she actually say *plain spinster*? Were mirrors scarce in the house where she was raised? She was very lovely. It was possible that her father scared away any potential suitors.

He had hoped she would stay with him and Daire. He could use Brynn to continue to keep house for him. Shaking his head, he sighed. It seemed like he only cared about himself.

"Hey, Cormac!" Bernie Harris greeted. "We were just figurin' how many stayed behind. It seems it was five."

"That's the number I arrived at. Any sign of them?"

"No." Bernie shook his head. "Look down the trail, too much dust being kicked up for it to be wagons. The herd should be here soon enough."

"Will we have to move?" Cormac asked.

"We've been informed by the captain that we are sufficiently off the trail and away from the grass they typically eat. It should be fine."

"Listen up!" The captain called out to get their attention. "It's customary to hold some festivities when two groups come together. Fun is fine, but no drinking and keep an eye on your ladies. These are saddle bums, and we know nothing about them. It's best to err on the side of caution."

"Cormac, you have two to keep track of," Sebastion Peterson commented. "It's just me and my wife." He didn't wait for a reply before he turned to Bernie. "You play the fiddle I hear. I can't wait to dance with the missus."

"We'll just take it by ear," Bernie replied.

Sebastian roared with laughter. "That was a good one, Bernie. Take it by ear and you play the music."

Bernie cocked his left brow and glanced at Cormac.

Cormac shrugged his shoulders before he turned away. He was on the verge of laughing, but didn't want to give the kid any encouragement. Sebastion looked too young to have a wife.

Walking back to the wagon, he shook his head. It was only a matter of time before trouble occurred. He'd just as soon not go, but Daire wasn't one to sit out a gathering.

CHAPTER EIGHTEEN

The music was lively, Bernie demonstrated his talent on the fiddle and Sebastian demonstrated his talent on the harmonica. Everyone knew the song Oh, Susanna. Daire and Brynn clapped their hands to keep time with the music.

"I've never danced before. It doesn't appear to be all that easy," Brynn said. Occasionally, the partners linked elbows, while at other times they held hands with a group of people. It looked as though everyone on the dance floor knew exactly how to dance.

"Once you see it a few times you get the gist of it. It can be quite fun. I'm not sure about this group of cowboys, though."

Despite having a stream not far away, they didn't seem to have made the effort to clean up. Dust swirled in the surrounding air. But they probably worked hard from sunup to sundown. Many unmistakably eating dust behind the cattle.

The frequent sideways looks toward them were a cause for concern. With her arms wrapped around her midsection, she purposefully avoided looking at any of them. Despite the no drinking rule, they stumbled a bit here and there,

"Where is Cormac?" Daire asked. Her anxiousness was evident in the high pitch of her voice.

He said he'd be back shortly, but then I saw Captain Browney take him aside. I hope the task he was given doesn't keep him away for too long."

Daire nodded. "At least you're married."

"I don't have a ring. I'm hoping for a peaceful night. The music is nice."

Daire smiled. "Bernie is wonderful. Who knew Sebastian had a talent. Oh, I didn't mean it that way, it's just he's ill-equipped for this journey."

We should stand closer to the brightness from the main fire. Sebastian's wife Thea is there," She suggested.

"So is Bea, but you're right we shouldn't be on our own. My concern was that if we moved closer, we might be expected to dance, but it appears that the party has evolved into a more spread out gathering. Daire linked arms with her, and they walked toward the party, skirting both dancers and cowboys.

Just keep focusing on the ground. Don't meet their eyes. I don't trust them," Brynn whispered.

"Me neither."

The short walk took longer than usual, but finally they reached the safety of the fire. They both nodded to the people from the wagon train.

"They have her tied to a bed in the wagon," Bea proclaimed, her voice booming.

Some women gasped, covering their mouths with their fingers as their eyes grew wider.

"I knew it! From the first glance, I knew she was trouble. The devil dwells inside of her!" an older woman named Wilma declared.

"Should we demand that she leave the wagon train?" Bea suggested.

Murmurs could be heard from the group. Too many heads nodded. The surrounding air grew uncomfortable.

"She must have escaped! She's dancing with a cowboy!" The group's focus shifted to where Bea was pointing.

"There's going to be trouble," Daire whispered as she took Brynn's hand. "Let's go back. I'd rather sit by our fire holding rifles then be a part of this."

Brynn didn't answer. They carefully weaved in and out of the people until they reached their wagon.

"Brynn, you're shaking! We'll be just fine. Let me grab a rifle."

Brynn sat on the ground next to the fire, waiting for Daire to grab the rifle from the front of the wagon. Shadows appeared before Daire returned.

"Howdy, little lady. It's sad to see you sitting here all by yourself," a disheveled man with few teeth said slowly.

"A shame," his sidekick echoed, spitting on the ground.

"Then it's a good thing I'm not alone." She stared beyond the fire, not wanting to be fire blind if she had to run into the dark.

"It's turned into a right ol' shindig. I'm Pen, and this here is Sonny. I think this is a right ol' song for us to dance to." His eyes narrowed when she didn't move.

"I thank you, gentlemen, but I don't dance." She sat up straight, trying to display confidence.

"First off, we ain't no gentlemen and second everyone dances. Don't force me to take you over to the party."

A wave of fear engulfed her. These men didn't have just a little elbow, hold hands and dance in a circle manner of dancing.

A rifle cocked behind her and her tension eased.

"I suggest you two get back. We don't want you here."

Daire stepped out from the front of the wagon with the rifle in her hands and the stock pressed against her shoulder.

"I wager she don't know how to use that thing," Sonny said before he chuckled.

"You're right Sonny. These men don't train their women to shoot. Now hand the gun over." Pen took a sinister step toward Daire.

She shot the ground in front of him, resulting in dirt flying up. Quickly, she reloaded and cocked the rifle. "I'm asking nicely. Please leave."

A small group of men, led by the captain, swiftly approached them.

"What in tarnation is going on here? No, don't answer I can already see you two saddle bums have been up to no good. Bernie and Hugo grab these guys and let's get them out of here." He waited until the cowboys had been hauled away and the crowd dispersed. "I'll get Cormac. I asked him to do some guard duty before the party started. I thought we'd need more men out there, but I can see now the danger is right here." Grumbling loudly, he walked away.

NEVER HAD his heart pounded so intensely. Racing across the circle of wagons, Cormac reached his sister and wife. Wife? When exactly did he start thinking of her in that way?

Daire ran into his open arms and wrapped her arms around his middle. Over the top of her head, his gaze captured Brynn's. He felt his heart ache at the fear in her eyes. He should have been here. He could have told the captain he had women to protect.

Daire sniffed, moved away, and mustered a weary smile. "I shot at one."

With his arm around her, he supported her as she found a

comfortable spot next to the fire. "What do you mean you shot one?"

"*At* one. I hit the dirt right at his feet. Pen's feet. He was getting ready to drag Brynn off. He had a friend with him. You didn't have to get close to smell the liquor on them, plus they were filthy. It was scary." Daire took a deep breath.

Cormac shifted his attention to Brynn. "Are you all right? Did they hurt you or did you shoot them too?"

A smile crossed Brynn's face. "No, I didn't have a gun. Your sister is a true hero. She saw them coming and snuck away to grab the rifle. I assumed we could just talk them into leaving but I was very wrong in that assumption. Pen's friend is Sonny, and yes, they were filthy. Pen asked me to dance, and I declined. I was rather polite but that didn't matter. I made the mistake of calling them gentlemen. Pen informed me he wasn't one and he was going to forcefully take me to the party. I knew that there were tough men, but they exceeded my expectations.

What had she imagined? Men with manners?

"I'm sorry I wasn't here. I should have at least told you where I was going." He sighed. "I thought you'd be fine by our fire. I won't repeat that mistake again.

"You'd best not. I'm going to bed," Daire told them. "Brynn, are you coming?"

"I'll be there in a minute. I'm still wound up. I won't be long."

Daire nodded before she climbed into the back of the wagon.

"Brynn, I really am sorry—"

"You have nothing to be sorry for. I'm ill-equipped to be out here in the wild. I'm completely unaware of the first thing about the world. My father accurately labeled me as a spinster. I'm not prepared for any other kind of life."

"First of all, you cannot be a spinster. You are married.

Second, how do you expect to know things when you haven't had the chance to experience them? Life is full of lessons at every step you take. Some lessons are good and others hard. You've seen beautiful sunrises and a substantial amount of Texas. You and Daire are as close as sisters and you've adapted well to life on the trail. You shouldn't wish to hide away because your father thought you should be a spinster. He simply aimed to prevent you from leaving him. I bet you did a lot to help him."

You're correct about my father wanting me to stay. Who else would work for free? I felt needed. But I do need to push ahead not believing I know nothing but exploring to see what I can learn."

Her smile beamed across the fire. Her face was even more breathtaking than he'd seen. Absent of fear, her eyes were captivating.

Glancing away, he frowned. Next, he'd be comparing her to a summer's day or a flower. He'd be in too deep if he wasn't careful. All there was to bear in mind was the fact that she was leaving.

Her clothes rustled as she stood. I'm heading to bed. Goodnight, Cormac."

He glanced at her and whispered, "Goodnight."

He looked away as she made her way to the wagon and got in. He knew better than to become entangled with a woman who wasn't willing to be his. He wasn't venturing down that path again. Not that Brynn was anything like Angela, but he'd end up with a heartache and no that wasn't happening again.

He hadn't reflected on Angela in months. They were engaged before the war and they wrote to each other, proclaiming their love, and she promised to wait for him. He had kept the letter she'd sent in which she wrote that she missed him beyond reason. It was merely two months old by the time he got it and another two weeks before he rode into town.

He had such high hopes, so many dreams. When he rode into town, he immediately noticed the whispers and the sympathetic gazes of the townspeople. He'd been well acquainted with them all of his life. After leaving his gelding, he immediately heard someone running on the boardwalk. He turned, expecting to see Angela, but it was Angela's friend Nancy, running toward him.

She stood in front of him, breathless. After a moment, she told him Angela had been married six weeks before to Sinclair Masters.

"The old banker?" He must have heard wrong.

"Cormac, I'm so sorry. She lives in a big house on the hill now. She owes you an explanation."

"She made her choice. I don't want to see her. Was she homeless or in dire straits?"

"We have all felt the impact of the war in one way or another, but no. Sinclair began courting her and he turned her head with all his gifts and attention. He had the house built for her." Nancy reached out and gently touched his arm.

"It must have happened quickly. I have a letter from her. She married a month after she shared with me that she loved me and would wait for me." The pit in his stomach became heavier by the minute.

This couldn't be happening. He lifted his hat off his head and ran his fingers through his hair before placing the hat back on.

"I'm going to ride out to the farm. I—"

"Cormac, your mother and sister aren't there. They are in a small town closer to San Antonio. Daire managed to secure a job there in a hospital. After both armies rode through, there wasn't much left of the farm. Daire was able to hide her horse. They stayed with my family for a week before they moved. I'm so sorry."

"Did the soldiers… Were my mother or sister hurt?" Breathing proved difficult.

"No, they weren't touched. What do you plan to do?"

Despite his rage, Nancy's innocent concern had a calming effect on him.

"I'm leaving. I can't stay here. People looked at me with pity when I arrived. It's best I move along."

"I understand. Sinclair gave your mother money for the land. Daire said it was a fair price and they'd be just fine."

"Thank you for the information, Nancy. I appreciate it. You take care."

He turned and heard her whisper, "You too."

CHAPTER NINETEEN

*H*ot and sweaty was one thing, but hot, sweaty and swarms of mosquitoes were another. The pests couldn't be deterred, no matter how many times they swatted them away. Only one more week. Brynn couldn't wait. Anxious about her unknown future and Cormac's avoidance, she felt overwhelmed.

At first, she thought it to be her imagination. Perhaps she had believed they were better friends than they were... If he'd said five words to her in the two weeks, that might be stretching the truth.

It made her heart ache. Her heart and head were not in sync. In fact, they were opposite. So many times, she had reminded herself that he was not her husband in truth. Her head understood, but her heart had a crack in it.

What had she done to make him so cold? It was as though he'd built a wall between them and then thickened the wall daily. Trying to just be a friend was too hard. It was as though she was an unwelcome visitor.

No, that wasn't it. She wasn't a visitor. Everyone pulled their weight. He never so much as uttered thanks when she'd cooked a meal or washed his clothes. He only acknowledged Daire when those things were done. It had grown dispiriting.

If only she understood the reason behind his abrupt detachment from her. He regretted marrying her, that much she knew.

She stumbled and righted herself.

"You all right?" Daire asked.

"I'm fine. Just not paying attention like I should."

I've noticed a difference in your mood recently. In fact, both you and Cormac have been difficult traveling companions. Grumpy at every turn, the both of you. Your silence and lack of smiles have been noticeable, and it's evident from your eyes that you're not happy. Are you sorry you made the trip with us?"

"Have I been taking my bad mood out on you? I'm sorry. I just don't know what I'm doing any more."

"It's my brother, isn't it?"

"I'm grateful for all you've done for me. I'm grateful to your brother too. I guess I'm too preoccupied with trying to understand why he won't talk to me or look at me. He ignores me. I tried to talk to him, but he walked away. I just want to understand why he dislikes me."

"Do you remember when you were in school and there was always a boy who pulled a girl's hair?" Daire asked.

"I remember a boy dipping my friend's hair in ink."

"Yes, my mother always told me the boys who like you are the ones who pull your hair or tease you." Her steps slowed and she turned her gaze upon Brynn. "I think Cormac has feelings for you."

Brynn sputtered and then burst into laughter. "If only it was that simple. It's my fault. I knew going into this that everything was an act. I never thought of us as married, but I sensed a closeness to him. I thought we were opening up to each other, getting to know each other." She shrugged. "I was wrong. He stopped speaking to me. I'm not experienced enough with friends to understand what I've done. He just walks away from me if you're not there. My emotions are getting battered." Taking a deep breath, she released it slowly.

"My pa was ornery, but I knew what to expect. He spent his days insulting and belittling me. I believed him and longed for him to stop reminding me of my flaws. My heart had grown cold over time. You've made so many friends on this trip while I... I just never have any idea what to say. Your brother's disregard for me is more bothersome than anything else."

Daire took her hand and gave it a quick squeeze then let go. "I noticed how he's been, too. I tried giving you two time alone, but every time I returned he was gone. I'm not sure what is happening with him. I genuinely believed he was interested in you and didn't want you to find out. It occurred to me that he might be trying to create some space because you are leaving. But it seems to be more than that. You didn't do anything. It's not your fault that he's grouchy."

Brynn smiled and nodded. Daire's well-meaning efforts to explain and provide comfort were unsuccessful.

They'd left the grassy plains behind and had been traveling through wooded areas for about a week. It would have been a pleasant change, if not for the mosquitoes. Even though the scenery was breathtaking, her worries remained.

A large portion of it must be the weariness she felt day after day. Why couldn't she put these feelings aside and just be grateful? Why was she unable to regain her happiness? Her bliss? Her excitement?

Lord, You must be tired of my constant prayers. They always seem the same lately. How do I find happiness? How do I overcome this hurdle in front of me? I do understand happiness isn't something to ask for. I need to let it all go and realize the beautiful world

You have made. I need to reexamine the wonder of it all. The wonder of Your love. Thank You, Lord.

She stopped to pick up a shiny rock on the ground and froze. The Indians were hiding among the trees.

Rapidly she caught up to Daire, seized her hand and yanked until she ran.

"Cormac! Indians!" she yelled.

Without hesitation, Cormac extended his arm and snatched Daire. As soon as Daire was up, he grabbed Brynn's arm and pulled. It felt like an eternity, but eventually she climbed onto the wagon and took the rifle from Daire.

"Get in the back!" Cormac yelled.

The horses were galloping as fast as possible, pulling the wagons to assemble in a circle. Quickly, everyone had sought refuge under the wagon, prepared to protect the group.

"Put your guns away, folks!" Captain Browney yelled. "They're here to trade."

Brynn collapsed on the ground. The only sound she heard for the next few seconds was the pounding of her heart. She should never forget that life was granted upon her as a precious gift from the Lord.

REACHING DOWN, Cormac aided Daire in escaping from under the wagon. Then he bent to help Brynn. His breath stalled in his lungs. He sensed a powerful connection that took his breath away.

He assisted her by placing his hand on her waist to help her up. It felt exceptionally good to be so close. He stepped aside and gathered the rifles.

"That was scary," Daire said in a shaky voice.

"It sure was," Brynn replied.

"You did the right thing, Brynn," he praised. "If it had been an attack your swift action would have saved us."

Brynn turned away, and he held back a sigh. He couldn't blame her. He was the one who pushed her away. Why did everything have to be difficult?

"What are they trading?" Brynn asked.

"All sorts of things. Anything from beads to deerskin dresses," he replied, pleased she was joining the conversation.

"What do they want in return?" Daire asked.

"We can go find out. Sometimes it's food, other times it's pots and pans. You never know."

Brynn shivered. "Is it safe? Maybe we should wait here."

Without answering, Cormac made his way to the area where everyone gathered, followed by the two women. As he moved closer, they maintained their distance. He couldn't blame them for being frightened.

Once the haggling was done, he walked back to his wagon, with Daire and Brynn following behind. He needed to obtain the items he intended to trade.

"You two can wait here if you like. I'm trading some beans and hardtack." He poured a significant quantity of both into sacks and took them to the area where everyone was actively involved in trading. It was just as well they stayed behind. The items he acquired were intended for them.

He was fully aware that he could have lost one or both today. He had behaved badly the last few weeks and had to make amends. Would a present mend the divide he'd created? He'd been unfriendly, but he couldn't help it. He'd constantly had the urge to sit down and talk with Brynn, but he had remained steadfast in his decision to avoid her. Now, his only option was to attempt to mend their relationship.

It was a chance worth taking. Throughout all the challenges, he came to understand the depth of his feelings for

Brynn. Pushing her away would be the biggest mistake of his life. Hopefully, she would forgive him for being so stubborn.

They had a fire ablaze and were already fixing supper. Daire and Brynn hadn't had a single argument in all the time they've been traveling. It was so different from some of the others in their group. Did they assume that yelling at each other inside the wagon meant nobody else could hear them?

The journey was exhausting, and tensions arose among the group. But not Brynn and Daire.

He moved nearer, and they directed their gazes toward him. He could see the questions in their eyes.

"Yes, these are for you." He handed them each a brightly colored Indian blanket. His heart expanded as they marveled over them.

"I have one more thing. I'm sorry for being difficult to get along with recently." He handed them each a beautifully crafted beaded necklace.

Despite their smiles, he was certain he noticed a glistening of tears in Brynn's eyes.

Daire sprang forward and hugged him. "Thank you. And yes, you have been a pain, but I forgive you." She let go and stepped back. "Brynn, why don't I put your blanket in the wagon?"

"That would be nice, thank you."

The silence was uncomfortable after Daire left.

Cormac racked his brain but came up empty.

Brynn appeared hesitant as she approached him. "Thank you, Cormac. I can't seem to remember getting presents before. The blanket is lovely, and the necklace is beautiful. Tears spilled down her cheeks.

Without a thought, he gathered her into his arms and held her. He should be horsewhipped for his behavior. Never a present? He knew things weren't pleasant when she grew up, but he'd never guessed.

"I'm sorry for treating you poorly. I allowed my past to dictate my behavior. Against my better judgment, I found myself getting close to you despite my vow to avoid relationships. Forgive me?"

Sniffling, she took a step back and nodded. "I'd like us to be friends again."

"I'd like that too." Although he wanted more, he would have to be patient. One step at a time.

CHAPTER TWENTY

fter many good-bye hugs and a few tears, they made their turn off and headed to the ranch. The tightness in Brynn's chest wouldn't subside, and she was worried about its severity. With each step, her feet became heavier and heavier. A pit formed in her stomach out of nowhere. Suddenly she had a realization.

It wasn't a medical problem; it was fear. Or maybe it was dread. Probably both. She'd had almost three weeks to develop a plan for her future and she'd failed. How far was the nearest town or homestead? Seeing the ranch and meeting Devlin was the right courteous thing to do. After that... Her posture drooped as her shoulders slouched. If she could find a job... How was she going to find one so far from town? At some point, she would have to move to town.

Worrying always brought more worries. She wanted to see the ranch and know how Cormac lived. What was Devlin like? Cormac never elaborated about either the ranch or his partner. And something would have to be done about their marriage. How exactly did one obtain annulment? What was once a simple idea had become a massive obstacle in her path.

God. She only had to put her trust in The Lord. Of course, she had faith in God. God was loving and always had her best interest at heart. The Lord set her on this path, and she was to follow.

Lord, how am I to know if I veer off the path? Trusting isn't the easiest thing. I will do my best. I trust You will guide me in the right direction. I've heard people say to give all worries to You. I will try my best, but I have a feeling I will still worry. And Lord? You might be hearing from me more than You're used to. Amen

She was so immersed in prayer, she failed to notice the wagon had stopped. She glanced up and saw Cormac's amused expression. How long had he been attempting to get her attention?

"You intending to walk while we ride?" Daire called to her from the seat next to Cormac.

Brynn's face became warm. "Of course not."

Before she could ask for help, Cormac reached out his arm to her. She took hold and laughed as she was swept up into the wagon. Daire moved over, creating an empty space in the middle. Daire tried to look innocent, but she wasn't fooling anyone.

Nestled between the siblings, Brynn smiled. "Let me know when we get to your land," she requested.

"We've been on it for about an hour. The road is just ahead, and the horses will be fine if we all ride together. Plus, the view is noticeably better from here. His gaze firmly fixed onto hers before he flicked the lines.

Was it possible for her face to become hotter? She must be so red. Apple red, she wagered. With a straight and tall posture, she endeavored not to make contact with Cormac in any way. But it became impossible to avoid occasionally bumping into each other. She and Daire bumped into each other just as much.

What a remarkable view! Rolling hills were adorned with trees and wildflowers. As the breeze gusted, the grass and flowers twirled together in a graceful dance. It wasn't long before she saw crops. She'd ask questions later. She couldn't distinguish one crop from another. In the opposite direction, she had a clear view of a vast expanse where cattle were feeding. She'd imagined something considerably smaller.

"Here's the house." There was no mistaking the pride in Cormac's voice.

And, oh… he had a right to be proud. There was a barn, a few other smaller buildings, and then the impressive house.

The log house was a beautiful two-story structure. Three maybe four times as big as what she had envisioned. There was a broad covered porch stretching along the front. There were a multitude of large windows. The magnitude of work and effort put into creating this place must have been extensive. Both edges of the house were lined with evergreens.

"It's beautiful!" It had her completely captivated.

"Come on, slow poke, let's explore the inside!" Daire called as she scrambled down the wagon.

Brynn moved to the side of the wagon Daire had climbed down. Cormac was there, all set to lend her a hand. He placed his hands on either side of her waist and lifted her down. Did his hands linger a few seconds longer than usual?

She needed to ignore such things before she turned apple red again.

As the door opened, a tall and exceptionally handsome man swiftly moved down the steps. He greeted Cormac with a big hug. "I was getting worried!"

"Took a bit longer than I planned." Standing beside the man, he gestured toward Daire.

"Devlin, this is my sister Daire." Daire was instantly enveloped in a hug.

"I feel as though I already know you. Cormac talks about you all the time."

"This is Brynn," Cormac introduced.

Hesitating, Devlin looked like he was sizing her up before embracing her briefly.

"Glad to make your acquaintance, Brynn. Or should call you Miss—"

"Mrs. O'Neill," Daire supplied.

Devlin frowned briefly. "Let's get you all inside."

———

DEVLIN FIXED his gaze on Cormac, studying him intently. Cormac raised his left shoulder and then let it fall.

He would explain it to his friend later. Not that there was a plan of what to say. It was hard to know what would happen next. The story had started out quite simple. But how would it end? Swallowing hard, he followed the others. He didn't want an ending.

They'd invested a lot of hard work building the ranch and the house. In preparation for his mother, sister, and potentially Devlin's someday wife, settling in, they had made it spacious.

"Cormac, this house is better than any we ever lived in. I know I can be happy here," Daire declared.

"What do you think, Brynn?" he asked. "Is it what you expected?"

"No, it's not at all what I pictured."

He frowned.

She shrugged. "I imagined a tiny shack with one window. You mentioned earlier that you and your partner built it, and

I figured you'd be so tired after ranching you wouldn't necessarily care where you slept."

Devlin laughed. We built the barn first and lived in it for a time while we constructed this. We had help at times. Ranchers around here are a good lot."

"One window? Is that so?" Cormac asked. His lips twitched.

"Yes, it's so. I'm totally in awe. A new stove too. This house is something a person could quickly grow accustomed to." She widened her eyes and then averted her gaze.

The uncomfortable tension heightened as both Devlin and Daire stared at him.

"Let's give you a tour upstairs," he suggested.

Devlin guided them up the stairs. "This one is mine," he gestured to the left. Cormac is across the hall. Daire, you can choose whatever you want and Brynn... Oh, never mind. As I said Cormac's room is this one." He opened the door for her.

"Brynn can pick any room she'd like. We have plenty for everyone," Cormac said. Devlin you can quit staring at me like that. We married so Brynn would be allowed to travel with us."

"Yes, I aided her escape from the asylum," Daire added with a grin.

"Cormac, can I have a word with you, outside?" Devlin asked.

Devlin hurried down the stairs and exited through the door. In an attempt to keep up, Cormac hustled after him.

"Asylum? Married? Separate rooms? Can you tell me what you were up to before you came here?" Devlin asked, his annoyance evident.

"Brynn was deposited at the asylum by a woman who claimed to be her mother-in-law. Brynn's father died and left her an inheritance. Daire wanted to help Brynn and rescued her from that dreadful place. Brynn needed to leave town before she was sent back into the asylum."

"Wait. Asylum as in crazy people? Did you sleep with one eye open every night? Crazy is something you don't want to mess with. And you married her?" Devlin shook his head.

"She is not crazy. She was a great help to Brynn during the trip. She is sweet and smart and caring—"

Devlin laughed. "You are infatuated with her. Are you positive the mother-in-law was not a real relation? Where was the alleged spouse? Wasn't it necessary for him to have his marriage papers in order to commit Brynn?"

"Apparently, you can commit a woman for various reasons, one of which is being lazy."

"Seriously? I'm glad she escaped, but marrying her? That's a major leap."

Cormac began walking toward the barn, with Devlin right by his side.

"I was wondering how long it would take before you headed to the barn. Winnie and her two-week-old filly are both doing well. Wait, hold up!"

Cormac heard Devlin's laughter behind him as he raced to the barn. Winnie was the finest horse he'd ever owned. She was a beautiful bay and exceptionally smart. The best part was she preferred him over Devlin.

Standing in front of her stall, Cormac couldn't control the smile spreading across his face. The filly looked just like her mother.

Winnie darted to the stall door and butted her head against Cormac's chest.

He chuckled as he stroked her face and glided his fingers along her neck. Winnie had been found on the ranch looking like a bag of bones. Cormac had fed her and showered her with gentle words until she trusted him.

"You did good, girl. Your baby is perfect. Did you know

she looks just like you? What do you think, will she be as smart?"

Winnie's head bobbed.

Devlin chuckled as he joined Cormac. "It was an easy birth. In fact, I walked into the barn and there was the foal. Winnie has reason to be proud."

"To think you didn't want to waste feed on 'Old Bones.'"

I made a mistake, but it was a singular occurrence. The rest of the time, I know what I'm talking about."

They both laughed.

"Brynn is staying with us for a while at least. The marriage is valid only on paper."

"Did a preacher preform the ceremony?"

"Yes, we were able to find one."

"Then the marriage is valid in the eyes of God."

Silence fell between the two of them.

"It's not up to me. I'm hoping she will stay, but we need to grow accustomed to one another. I really like all I know so far, but traveling in a wagon is different than living in a house. Since she's never been on a farm or ranch, we'll need to be patient with her as she learns. Daire's a good teacher."

"Did she help on the trip?"

"Yes, she's a good worker and she learns fast. She'll be an asset to the ranch. You'll see."

"I trust your judgment," Devlin assured.

"I'd best get them settled in. You coming?" Cormac asked.

"I'm going to chop some wood first. See ya."

They walked in opposite directions. Devlin was usually reasonable. His questions about Brynn were unexpected. Hopefully, it wouldn't prove to be a problem.

CHAPTER TWENTY-ONE

"*I* love the scent of the house, a mix of wood and cedar. It's even better than I expected," Brynn said to Daire while they settled into their adjacent rooms. "I wasn't sure what we'd ride up to. They put this ranch together rather quickly. I was expecting to learn how to use a hammer and nails." She laughed softly.

Daire joined in.

"I'm finished, we might as well explore the kitchen," Brynn suggested.

"Yes. I want to see what provisions they have. There are still plenty in the wagon. Devlin seems nice don't you think?" Daire smiled. "He is rather handsome. I hear he's unmarried. That's a bonus for you," Brynn teased.

"I'm waiting for love," Daire proclaimed. "Love that captures your heart and never releases it. You wouldn't know anything about that would you, Brynn?" Daire's lips twitched.

"I have no idea what you mean."

As they walked down the stairs, Brynn's eyes widened at the sight of Cormac waiting for them.

Their eyes met, and she immediately sensed a wave of emotion from him. Something was different about him. Where was the usual, *we're friends but you're still leaving* air he usually gave out? With a single glance, that man had her twisting and turning.

Walking away, she entered the spacious kitchen. It was either all or none with Cormac. Daire's words of love that captured the heart repeated in her mind. She'd need to pray on this.

"What do you know! Brynn, come and see what's in the pantry."

Brynn immediately hurried to her friend's side. They stood and stared. Lined up neatly on the shelves were glass jars filled with meat, vegetables, and fruits. There were plenty of staples too, including a block of sugar and a wheel of cheese.

"I've never seen such an abundance of food. Cormac, you didn't jar all this did you?" Daire asked.

Cormac laughed. "No, we bought what we could. This being our first winter we knew we'd be short on food. There hadn't been enough time to put up hay and store food for us. We decided to put up as much hay as we could, then we headed to Fort Worth and stockpiled food. If you need something we didn't get, Devlin plans to take a trip there in a few weeks."

"I doubt we'll need anything," Brynn told him. She faced him. "Are the jars arranged by food type and in alphabetical order? Cormac, surely you didn't do this."

"You doubt my ability to arrange food?"

"You probably can but it's the alphabetical order. I can't picture you doing it that way." She smiled and enjoyed his smile in response.

"You'd be right about that. I caution you against purpose-fully rearranging anything. A fight could break out."

The front door closed. "A big ol' fight with bruises left."
After staring at each person, Devlin finally nodded.

"Bruises?" Daire asked. She sounded confused.

"Just a few," Cormac replied.

"A few black eyes," Devlin added. "We each sported one.
The supplies have not been out of order since."

Brynn turned her head and caught Daire's gaze. Both
lifted their brows. Definitely a matter worth noting.

"Why don't you men do whatever you do, and we'll get
supper made?" Daire suggested. She didn't pause for an
answer. She stepped into the pantry and grabbed a few jars,
set them on the counter, and then grabbed a few more.

"I could light the stove for you," Devlin offered.

Daire appeared flustered. "I can do it."

Brynn glanced at Cormac, and they both erupted into
laughter. Once Devlin cast them the evil eye, they stopped
right away.

"I suppose we can find something to do," Devlin said. He
walked to the door and waited for Cormac to join him. They
stepped outside.

Daire crossed her arms in front of her. "I don't like being
teased."

"I'm sorry. When I glanced at Cormac, it was obvious he
was about to burst into laughter, and I couldn't help but
join in."

"Mmhmm." Daire nodded. "Let's get this food started. I
want to make peach cobbler. I haven't seen so much sugar
before."

"FUNNY, you and your woman are truly humorous."

Cormac cocked his brow. "My woman? It was funny. I'm

sorry. I glanced at Brynn, and she just started laughing. I couldn't help it."

Devlin gave him a long stare. "Right. We could stack the wood closer to the house. A few more months and it'll start getting cold."

"Not as cold as those folks in the north," replied Cormac. "I listened to them describe the snow and ice. One fella said the snow was so high it was over his head. We'll be ready for the little bit of snow we might experience. When you go to town, ask if any of the men have read the Farmer's Almanac. That has reliable predictions of how bad the winter will be."

"I'm uncertain if those tales are believable. That sounds like an incredible amount of snow. I'll check around for an almanac when I get to town. I'm leaving in three days," Devlin told him.

Cormac nearly dropped the load of wood he was carrying. "I thought you were going in a couple weeks."

"That would have been accurate if you had gotten back earlier." He shrugged. "I need tobacco."

"Why don't you stop with the tobacco? Did you see some of those soldier's teeth? Rotted."

Devlin shook his head. "Maybe next time. This time I'm getting tobacco. I won't get as much and by the time I'm out it'll be too cold to make a trip to town for more. Besides, who made you my mother?"

"Someone has to look out for you. I'm not sure that makes me your mother, though. A concerned friend is what I am. If I can quit whiskey, you can quit tobacco. However, you're correct, you're completely grown up now."

"That I am. Will Brynn be joining me? I could put her up at the boarding house for a week. She should be able to find a job by then." Devlin shot him a sideways glance.

"Trying to stir up trouble?" Cormac sighed. "Honestly, I had hoped for more time, but I'll talk to her before then."

"Sounds like a plan, my friend."

CHAPTER TWENTY-TWO

*L*earning about Devlin's imminent departure in two days had left her feeling completely deflated. It was as if her heart had been torn out while being kicked in the stomach.

Pretending to be fine and acting as though she was excited to leave... How was she supposed to accomplish that? She'd hidden her feelings from her father, but this was different. Very different. Could she be whole without Cormac?

Looking from her bedroom window, she watched Cormac chop wood. Where would she be this winter? Would she still be in Texas? Perhaps Cormac will meet a wonderful woman and marry her. Most likely someone attractive and not socially awkward. Even in her imagination, she struggled to envision herself being sociable and effortlessly mingling with others.

Spinsters weren't meant to marry. She shouldn't have let herself believe that there was even a possibility with a man like Cormac. He was kind and generous. He gave before he took. When he asked for her opinion, she believed he genuinely wanted to hear her thoughts.

How could she possibly believe that what she had to say was valid? It's likely that her father was watching over her and laughing.

With a sigh, she moved away from the window and sat down at the foot of her bed. She had deluded herself into thinking she could feel his love, even though he'd never expressed it. How embarrassing. She must have been pining over him, making him uncomfortable. How had she failed to realize...

At least there wasn't much to pack. She owned her shoes, the blanket, and the beautiful necklace Cormac had given her. Fingering the necklace, her fingers shook. He gave his sister a blanket and necklace, too. He was simply being kind to a spinster.

She'd heard plenty about spinsters making fool of themselves trying to find a husband. The old widows she'd had to sit with hadn't always been kind. However, everyone felt sympathy for the old maids. She'd told Cormac she'd marry a man who wanted her. Why had she assumed she'd be wanted or needed even?

She fell to her knees, clasping her hands together.

Lord, thank You for keeping us safe. It is by Your grace I am here, and I should be happy to continue on the path You have provided me. No path is easy, is it? I will walk down Your path and I will be grateful. I am grateful. You have created the most glorious place. You are in every tree, every mountain, every person. I will keep my eyes open for every lesson life has to teach me. Your will be done. I have faith in You, Lord. I feel the love You have for me, and I thank You with everything in me. My life belongs to You. Thank You God, amen.

SHE WAS EMBRACED by a gentle calmness that wrapped around her. There would be happy times and times of devas-

117

tation, but through it all, God would be with her. His path was the path she would follow. How exactly wasn't clear, but she had faith.

———

CORMAC WIPED the sweat off his face with his bandanna. The glimpse of Brynn's devastated face had cut him deep. He'd tried to engage in conversation with her the previous night and again at breakfast, but she showed no interest. She'd been that way ever since Devlin announced his plan to leave soon.

He'd be happy if she called him sugarplum again. How ridiculous was that? He was a cowboy. He was tough. Well, maybe not always. He didn't feel so tough now. It was her choice. From the beginning, the plan was to obtain an annulment. He just got carried away.

It was better to know now. Was it him she wasn't interested in? Or ranch life? Both? He'd thought Angela had hurt him. But it was more like she had wounded his pride. The current heartache he was feeling was markedly dissimilar. *You can't make someone love you if they don't.* It was that simple.

The front door closed, and he turned around.

"I thought you'd be out here," Daire said.

"Looking for me, were you?" The only thing he could muster was a quick smile.

"Brynn is crying. She doesn't want to leave."

"Did she say that, Daire? Did she say those words?" His stubborn heart still held hope.

"Not exactly. She hasn't talked to me at all. She did say she was tired and need to rest up—"

"So, she can leave tomorrow," he finished. He removed his hat and smacked it against his thigh. "I don't want to see her. I'll be checking on the cattle for most of the day. If she does poke her head out of her room be sure to tell her I will pay for a room at the boarding house for as long as she needs."

"You could try…"

He scowled.

"Never mind. See you when you get back." Daire walked back into the house.

Why wasn't Brynn talking to Daire? That was a first. He smashed his hat back on and headed for the barn. He had cattle to check on. Maybe he should plan to spend the night out there. Shaking his head, he dismissed the idea. No woman was going to control his actions.

CHAPTER TWENTY-THREE

he experience of sitting at the supper table was far from comfortable. She had planned to be polite, join the group, and then head back to her room. But Devlin and Daire had other ideas.

"You'll need to take more dresses than you packed," Daire told her.

"I packed two, and I thank you for all you've given me. You all have been very generous to me." She ducked her head down again, hoping to be left alone.

"I hope the cattle were still there," Devlin said.

"Why wouldn't they be?" Cormac asked, unable to keep the hint of irritation out of his voice.

"Just making conversation," Devlin replied.

"We're having nice weather," Daire said.

Brynn looked up and stared at both Daire and Devlin for a while.

"We've established that the cattle are where they are supposed to be. I have enough dresses and the weather is nice. What shall we talk about next?"

"I didn't mean to rile you, Brynn. It's just that you and

Cormac don't seem to be talking, and Daire and I are filling in the silence with whatever words come to mind." Devlin smiled. It was an innocent smile, but she knew better.

"What are you two up to?" The irritation in her voice was impossible to hide.

"No need to be rude to them," Cormac remarked while staring at her.

"I—I'm sorry. I didn't intend to come across as rude. If you'll excuse me. Daire, let me know when to do the dishes." She stood up, donned her wrap, and headed toward the front door. Fresh air and time alone was what she needed.

Cormac offered, "Allow me," as he opened the door, causing her to jump once again.

"Thank you. I'll be fine by myself."

"I reckon you think that to be the truth, but I'm not fine and I need to talk to you." His tone brooked no refusal.

WITH A FIERY GAZE, she walked outside before him. After taking a deep breath, he stepped out and closed the door.

She was obviously trying to look mad, defiant perhaps, but it wasn't working. She had transformed from a confident woman to someone who was scared of her own shadow, right in front of him.

He wanted to reassure her, but he didn't know what her future held.

"Let's have a seat." He gestured to the chairs on the porch. Relief filled him when she sat down.

"We were the best of friends a few days ago. You are Daire were like sisters, and today you wouldn't speak with her. I wish you'd talk to me and tell me what is bothering you. I don't want us to part like this." He hoped she'd unfold her arms and relax.

"It's the parting. I'll miss you all. I'm just not good at goodbyes." Her words lacked sincerity.

"Goodbyes aren't always forever. It'll break Daire's heart if you don't plan to see her once in a while. I'm curious about what you have in mind for your future." If only she would say that she planned to stay.

"I'm going to look for a job."

"There aren't many jobs in town for women. What type of job were you hoping to find?"

She blinked a few times. Was she flustered?

"I'm not quite sure. I thought I could work at the diner or maybe I could be a teacher. I am well educated."

"There isn't a diner. The town is small. They serve food in the saloon, but that isn't a place for a decent woman. And a teacher was hired for this school year. Unless she had to leave, I doubt that job is available."

"I thought I could try to find a job in another town if I had to or—"

"No."

Her eyes widened. "No? I didn't finish what I was going to say. What entitles you to tell me what I can or cannot do? I was going to say I would find a husband." The expression on her face began to crumple. "Never mind, I know that won't happen. I'll be fine." Her voice carried a heavy weight of sadness.

"Never mind? Are you still under the impression that nobody would want to marry you? I thought we talked about this before."

"I'm a bitter spinster. Ill-tempered even."

"Ill-tempered?"

"I must confess, I wasn't the most courteous person today." She quickly averted her eyes.

If only he could read her mind. Her plan wasn't a very sound one.

"What about the annulment? How are you going to manage it?"

She swiftly turned her head, and their gazes met.

"I thought you'd take care of it. I intend to keep our marriage a secret from everyone. I'll use my maiden name."

"What if the Thistles are looking for Brynn Walsh? What then?" He couldn't help the loudness of his voice. She was risking her own safety.

"I don't want to argue with you, Cormac." She sighed.

He stood. "Come with me. I have something in the barn I want you to see."

She hesitated before nodding.

He extended his hand and felt relief when she accepted it.

CHAPTER TWENTY-FOUR

*U*pon arriving at the barn, she wrapped herself in her shawl and gazed up at Cormac. "Well, what's this all about?" While walking to the barn, countless ideas had raced through her mind. The most logical one was to continue the discussion about the annulment. She attempted to brace herself for more of his doubts about her plans, but her heart had already dropped.

"Devlin is heading to town in the morning. We need talk about what we are going to do."

She looked away from him and acted captivated by the hay. "Do? I already explained my plans."

Sorrow swept through her as the silence lingered.

"It's imperative we make the right decision for both of us. I know we had an agreement, that we made the promise to annul our marriage before we even got to know each other. Devlin reminded me that we made a vow to God on our wedding day."

She studied his face. There wasn't a hint of his feelings in his expression.

"Is that the only reason the annulment would trouble you?"

"No. It is concerning, though." He extended his hand once more, and she took it.

They proceeded deeper into the barn and then stopped at a horse stall. Stepping forward, she covered her heart with her hand. "Is that a baby horse?"

He smiled at her. "This is Winnie, my mare, and her new filly. I haven't named her yet. In a roundabout way I'm saying I want what they symbolize. They are the future of the ranch. Children will be the future of the ranch."

"Oh, you want children." Would any woman do?

"Yes, I want children with you."

"For the future of the ranch."

He took off his hat and ran his fingers through his hair. "I'm not good at talking about feelings. I would prefer it if you stayed right here, married to me. In all honesty, I had no intention of finding a wife. When I was a soldier, I thought I had a sweetheart, but a month after she told me she loved me she married another man. It was a long journey to heal from the hurt and humiliation." He took her other hand too. "Little did you know, you've settled deep within my heart. There is so much about you I admire. First of all, I find you very beautiful."

"Cormac—"

"Don't interrupt me. I have to get this all out. Your personality is characterized by generosity and kindness. You are not ill-tempered. You are always eager to lend a hand. I don't think you'd be too lonely way out here. Daire is here. I hold immense respect for the person you are, and above all else, Brynn, I love you."

Despite tears streaming down her face, she succeeded in smiling. He wasn't sending her away. Relief shrouded her, and all her stored-up feelings came to the surface. "I didn't want to go. I didn't know how to tell you I wanted to be your wife. I've never felt safer or more appreciated before. I made an effort not to love you, but like you, I couldn't suppress my feelings. Once they began, they continued to grow, and I can honestly say I love you, Cormac."

His expression changed from disbelief to relief to happiness. He smiled and pulled her close, wrapping his arms around her.

"So, I'm not leaving," she murmured.

"No chance of that," he murmured back.

There was an undeniable sense of rightness in being wrapped in his arms. He exceeded all her hopes for an ideal partner. He was both good and kind, consistently putting others' needs ahead of his own. Above all, he cherished her and had faith in God.

"Shall we name the filly?" he asked.

"How about Destiny?" she suggested.

Taking a step back he smiled at her. "Perfect, absolutely perfect." He pulled her to him for a kiss.

EPILOGUE

*B*rynn wandered out to the front porch to join her husband. The way his face brightened whenever he saw her made her heart glow. The confidence she possessed was beyond anything she'd imagined.

Cormac stretched out his arm towards her and gently pulled her onto his lap.

"What are Devlin and Daire arguing about this time?" he asked, looking amused.

"The food in the pantry is out of alphabetical order. The funny part is Daire didn't do it. I'm not sure if anyone warned Grady about the possibility of a black eye if he messed up the order of the contents in the pantry. She placed her head on his shoulder. "We'll have to clue him in. I was glad when you told Daire and me. Black eyes are serious. Where is Grady?"

"He went to town to get his claim sorted. The map he saw and the map he was given are not the same. Either way his land will still butt up against ours. I think it's an excellent idea to combine the land with ours. Three men working a larger ranch will give us all additional profit."

Caressing his chin, she nodded. "There are two women working too." Cormac never once denied her any request. Even though she didn't ask for much. Lately it's been yard good, buttons and yarn.

"Are you angling for more cloth for dresses?" he teased.

"No, I have plenty for dresses. I'm going to teach Daire how to sew her own dresses. Daire promised to teach me how knit." She couldn't suppress her excitement.

They watched as Grady rode in. He dismounted and gave them a nod. He had to be the most towering man around. He leisurely walked to the porch and climbed the few steps.

"What are you two lovebirds doing?" he asked.

"First of all, I'm the love bird, Cormac is sugarplum. Before you snicker, I have a warning for you."

His brow furrowed. "What would that be?"

Devlin likes, actually he demands that everything in the pantry is placed in alphabetical order. He is so emphatic about it he once caused sugarplum to have a black eye."

"I gave him one back, but I learned not to tamper with the pantry. In fact, he's accusing Daire of the mess."

"Taking a jar, looking at it and moving it to a different spot is a mess? You waited until I sorted out my claim to tell me, didn't you? Were you afraid I'd come to the conclusion that being partners with you and Devlin would be too odd?" He grinned.

"I'll go in and take the blame." Grady sighed.

"A big, really big apology would avoid a black eye," she warned before she laughed.

Grady opened the door and stepped inside.

"Odd? Brynn love of my life, do you consider me odd?"

"How can I say yes when you add *love of my life* to the question?" She grinned and stood up. "Come on, let's go for a walk before any fighting takes place."

"So, you do consider me odd?" Cormac stood and strolled down the steps with Brynn.

"I didn't believe so, but perhaps I could discover a few peculiarities about you."

Cormac took her hand. "I'd much rather you think of all the ways you love me instead."

They strolled for a bit, then stopped. He faced her. "I thank God every morning and every sunset that you are my wife. You have helped to restore my faith."

Her face heated. "I'm so pleased. My faith had deepened since putting up with, I mean since I met you."

They continued walking.

"Minx," he remarked.

"Sugarplum," she said.

THANK you for reading Spinster No More!

For a Special Excerpt download *Spinster No More Five Years Later*. You can find it at https://dl.bookfunnel.com/v4j7lkj7o6

If you loved this book, you won't want to miss the McKeegan series—each story is a captivating journey of romance, faith, and adventure!" **My Book**

In a story of faith, courage, and love's resilience, *Aiden, The McKeegans* weaves a gripping tale of family secrets, buried regrets, and the undeniable pull of a love destined to be. Will Eireann and Aiden find the strength to embrace their true feelings, or will the shadows of the past keep them apart?

Dive into this emotionally charged Christian Historical Western Romance by USA Today Bestselling Author Kathleen Ball, and experience a saga that will make you laugh, cry, and believe in the power of love and faith.

ABOUT THE AUTHOR

Kathleen Ball is an USA Today Bestselling Author who pulls her readers into each story. She loves to write about flawed characters and how they change for the better. Her books have happy endings, it's the story of getting there that enchants her readers.

Visit my website Kathleenballromance.com

facebook.com/kathleenballwesternromance
x.com/kballauthor
instagram.com/author_kathleenball
tiktok.com/@kathleenballromance
amazon.com/author/kathleenball

OTHER BOOKS BY KATHLEEN

Mail Order Brides of Texas set

Cinder's Bride

Keegan's Bride

Shane's Bride

Tramp's Bride

Poor Boy's Christmas

Oregon Trail Dreamin' set

We've Only Just Begun

A Lifetime to Share

A Love Worth Searching For

So Many Roads to Choose

The Settlers set

Greg

Juan

Scarlett

Mail Order Brides of Spring Water Set

Tattered Hearts

Shattered Trust

Glory's Groom

Battered Souls

Faltered Beginnings

Fairer Than Any

Romance on the Oregon Trail Set

Cora's Courage

Luella's Longing

Dawn's Destiny

Tara's Trial

Candle Glow and Mistletoe

The Kavanagh Brothers set

Teagan: Cowboy Strong

Quinn: Cowboy Risk

Brogan: Cowboy Pride

Sullivan: Cowboy Protector

Donnell: Cowboy Scrutiny

Murphy: Cowboy Deceived

Fitzpatrick: Cowboy Reluctant

Angus: Cowboy Bewildered

Rafferty: Cowboy Trail Boss

Shea: Cowboy Chance

Mail Order Brides of Pine Crossing set

Alanna

Briana

Aggie

The McKeegans

Aiden

Brayden

Myles

Caden

Nolan

A Cowboy's Chance

Burke's Sweet Beloved

Clint's Sweet Calamity

Sweet Lasso Springs

Garrett

Stamos

Stetson

Sweet Cowboy Seasons

Summer's Cowboy

Autumn's Cowboy

Winter's Cowboy

Spring's Cowboy

Non Series Books

Snowbound Hearts